Key to Kashdune

BY CLAUDIA WHITE

Key to Kashdune

BY CLAUDIA WHITE

MP PUBLISHING

First edition published in 2014 by
MP Publishing Limited
Queens Promenade
12 Strathallan Crescent
Douglas, Isle of Man IM2 4NR British Isles
mppublishingusa.com

White, Claudia.
Key to Kashdune / by Claudia White.
p. cm.
ISBN 1-84982-231-2
Summary : Melinda and the Huttons discover the magical island of
Kashdune, where Athenites live freely. They must stop their old nemesis,
Professor Stumpworthy, from seizing power on the island and tearing their
family apart.

[1. Mythology, Greek --Fiction. 2. Shapeshifting --Fiction. 3. Family
--Fiction. 4. Siblings --Fiction. 5. Fantasy fiction.] I. Title.

[Fic] --dc23
Jacket Design by Alison Graihagh Crellin
Jacket Image by Larissa Kulik

ISBN-13: 978-1-84982-231-2
10 9 8 7 6 5 4 3 2 1

Also available in eBook

To Thurman and Claire White,
my wonderful parents.

CHAPTER ONE

The torch beam searched the walls of the dark and humid cavern. Harmony's hand trembled as the light wavered; the batteries were losing power. Just being in a cave was enough to trouble her. Nothing in her ten years as both a doctor and a teacher could have prepared her for this. But it wasn't just the darkness and the silence that made her tense; all her survival instincts were screaming at her to flee. She swallowed the feeling and continued exploring the remains of what had been one of the most extraordinary archaeological finds of its day. There was little left since Horace Stumpworthy had demolished the hieroglyphs. The mere thought of such destruction of priceless history made her blood boil.

Harmony and her uncle, Joe Whiltshire, had arrived in Turkey less than a month before. They spent most of the month organizing and surveying the area where the cave was supposed to be. When they located it, they worked day and night for six days, desperately hoping to find a trace of Joe's earlier discovery. More than ten years before, Joe, who had been working in the area as an archaeologist, discovered the cave after an earthquake cleared the rubble from the entrance. The walls inside had been covered in rich, informative drawings that detailed the existence of Athenites, a race of people that could take the shape of other animals—Harmony and Joe's ancestors. More importantly, the cave drawings told the story of peaceful coexistence between humans and their unique Athenite cousins. But Horace Stumpworthy had done all he could to destroy them, and little remained of the beautiful hieroglyphs.

Harmony tensed again, her animal senses telling her to move, to get out of the cave as fast as possible. She tried to ignore the impulse, but this time she couldn't quiet her fear. She yelled for Joe to run. Joe stood motionless for an instant, trying to understand what Harmony was shouting about. Then the earth above and below them started to shake.

"Get out of here!" Harmony yelled over her shoulder. Her uncle was already running close behind her.

"That tremor could bring the whole place down!" Joe called as they ran toward the cave entrance.

The earth groaned and growled, then shifted again, bringing down a rain of rocks over their heads. Another tremor unleashed stones the size of watermelons that crashed horrifyingly close, sending Harmony and Joe scrambling for safety. Dust clogged the air, blocking out the light through the narrow opening. The brightness of the entrance vanished and they watched as the opening dissolved before them. Only seconds passed in what seemed like an endless nightmare before they were left in total darkness.

Thousands of miles away, in North America, eleven-year-old Melinda Hutton waited for the dust to settle before struggling to her feet. Her body transitioned back to her human size; her beak was replaced with a mouth and curly reddish-brown hair topped her head again. But not all of her body responded so smoothly to the change: feathers still clung to her cheeks, her arms were still shielded inside wings and, although her feet had grown to their full human size, they were still very claw-like and scaly.

Melinda's first flight had been a success; her first landing, nearly disastrous. She had come in too fast and at too steep an angle. She had pushed with her wings as her father instructed, but the speed of her descent made the movement difficult. Her wings caught the wind, bringing her body up slightly, but not enough and not in time. It wasn't much of a landing. It was more like she was the ball and the ground the bat as she hit the grass, then ricocheted back into the air. Her next confrontation with the earth sent her into an uncontrollable spin and she somersaulted several yards away. The whole thing was over very quickly, but as Melinda felt each bump, spin, and tumble, she wondered if it would ever end.

Transforming into different animals had become almost second nature for Melinda over the past several months. She'd only learned about her Athenite heritage a year before, but she practiced her skills every day. Athenites could take the form of any animal, eventually learning to use the skills of that animal as if they were born that way. All it took was concentration, much like a human learning to walk, throw a ball, or ride a bike. Melinda had gotten quite good at many of her transformations and would have been able to master them all if she could learn to concentrate on what she was doing. More often than not her mind would wander and she would change into an impossible creature made up of different animal parts, like a rabbit with a rat's tail and goat's hooves or a pony with feathers. This beast would often sport Melinda's freckled face and beaver-like smile.

Today her father, Jake, had decided to teach her how to transform into a bird and fly. At the onset, he seemed like the perfect teacher because of his calm manner. Nothing ever seemed to ruffle or rile him. This was probably because, as a doctor of human and animal medicine, he had seen things that would make most people scream, cry, faint, or at least cringe. Not Jake Hutton—he always kept his cool. His dark hair was always neatly combed straight back, his dark-rimmed glasses always rested comfortably at the bridge of his thin nose, and he always held his lean body tall and straight. He never showed any of the classic signs of stress no matter what was happening around him. Until his daughter tried to fly, that is.

"Okay then," he had said, biting his lip in frustration, "let's try it again. Unlike a crawling insect or mammal, a bird must be *precise*." Jake pushed his glasses back in place with a shaking hand. "You can't have a hawk's beak on a sparrow-sized head, huge goose feet and hummingbird wings on a…a…a…" He paused when he realized that he had no idea what type of bird Melinda had imagined when she styled her body. He shook his head and sighed. "You look ridiculous." He paused again as he smoothed his hair back off his forehead. "You'll never get off the ground that way. Don't just think *bird*…picture the one you want to be."

Melinda eyed her father as she tried in vain to put a pout on her beak. She was quite certain that she looked perfectly bird-like. He was right about one thing, however, and that was that no matter how hard she flapped her tiny wings, she could not lift off the ground. She transformed back to human form to begin the process again.

Luckily a kestrel glided overhead then, directly above them. Melinda was overwhelmed by its beauty and closed her eyes, absorbed in the sensations of transformation. Her skin tingled as feathers sprouted; her arms felt light, almost weightless. Her skin tightened and stretched across a bony framework that was light and strong and her arms disappeared inside wings. When the sensations had passed, she opened her eyes and stared at her father's shoes.

Jake felt incredibly relieved as he looked down at the beautiful kestrel at his feet. "You did it, kiddo! You made it! You're perfect!" Then he closed his eyes and calmly transformed into a slightly bigger kestrel. He looked nervously at his daughter, wondering how this next phase of her education—which was really the most difficult and dangerous—was going to turn out. "Ready then," he said, trying desperately to put a little enthusiasm in his tone, "let's try out those wings."

Melinda felt awkward as she opened her wings. Each was longer and broader than her entire body. She raised and lowered them slowly, feeling the pressure as she pushed against the air. It didn't take her long to get the hang of it, and seconds later she was airborne. Her flight lasted only a few seconds before she tipped forward and slammed into the dirt, unfortunately beak first. She tried again. This time she propelled herself a little bit higher for a little bit longer before losing her balance.

"That's it," Jake cringed.

Melinda eyed him in disbelief. "Surely this isn't really it!" she hissed, spitting out the sandy dirt that was caked inside her beak.

"Now this time, hold your head up high, tighten your back muscles—like this—and you'll be flying." Jake swung his wings together with precise momentum and rose into the air.

"I can do this," Melinda whispered. "If I can change into one of these things, I can fly, too." Intensifying her concentration and using huge whooshing sweeps of her wings, she began to rise into the air. Higher and higher she propelled herself until the house and trees were in the distance.

"That's the way," Jake called with a nervous quiver in his voice. "Now slow down and keep your wings out. Just relax and glide."

Melinda did so. Suddenly she felt a freedom she'd never known. It was as if the air was holding her, both pushing and pulling while its gentle, massaging fingers rippled through her feathers.

They'd flown only a short distance when Jake called again, "It's time to go back. I want you to watch my landing carefully. It's not as easy as it looks," he said as he swooped gracefully toward the ground.

Melinda followed, diving a little too sharply. It didn't feel like flying anymore as she plummeted toward the ground.

"NOW, MELINDA! NOW! USE YOUR WINGS!" Jake screamed at the sight of his daughter's free fall.

That was the last thing she'd heard as she careened across the lawn. Then came the crash, and the tumble, and the sprawling roll. Finally resting on her back, she waited for the shrieks of concern from her father. Instead, she heard wails of laughter from her brainy thirteen-year-old brother, Felix, who had just returned from his home away from home: the library.

Jake was instantly at her side, and after a quick examination to make sure that she was still alive, he sighed. "Don't worry, Melinda, you'll get the hang of all this without a problem—well, without more problems." Melinda sulkily rolled onto her front, feathers and dust whirling around her head.

Felix calmly readjusted his thick black glasses that, as usual, had slipped down his pointy nose. He was dressed in his favorite black jeans and black t-shirt picturing a winking Albert Einstein on the front. His choice of clothing did nothing to enhance his tall, skinny frame. With his bushy dark brown hair topping his head, he looked a bit like an overused rag mop. "Awesome landing, Mel," he groaned, more convinced than ever that he would never willingly learn the skills of an Athenite, having never suffered even the slightest fantasy about transforming into anything. "I'll go inside and see if you made the six o'clock news," he teased, before spinning around and disappearing inside the house while Melinda attempted to transform back to human form.

Jake's shoulders sagged as he witnessed Melinda's failed attempt to totally eradicate her feathers and return to her ten-toed human feet. "Melinda, you seem more distracted than usual today. What's up?"

Melinda looked up then followed her father's gaze to her huge kestrel feet. "I can't seem to concentrate," she sighed. "Ever since I got up this morning, I haven't been able to get Joe and Harmony out of my mind."

"Why is that?"

Before Melinda could answer, Felix came bounding back out of the house. "Dad, it's horrible! I just saw on the news that there's been an earthquake in Turkey—right where Joe and Harmony are working!"

CHAPTER TWO

The news of the earthquake came as a shock—not to the world, just to the Huttons. With no reports of casualties or property damage, the world's news agencies quickly moved on to a story about a pop star who'd recently dyed his hair in pink and yellow stripes. No one except the Huttons seemed to care about the seismic disturbance in Turkey. After two painful weeks with no word from their friends Joe Whiltshire and Harmony Melpot, the Huttons decided to take matters into their own hands.

Following a hastily organized trip, a very long flight from America to Turkey, and an even longer drive through the hot desert landscape, Melinda, Felix, and their parents, Elaine and Jake, arrived in the uninspiring village of Assos. The surrounding countryside was peaceful and almost uninhabited, with the exception of a handful of small farm dwellings and roaming herds of livestock. Civilization had mostly ignored the area.

"This is disgusting," Felix whimpered as they parked in front of the seedy-looking, paint- peeling, dilapidated Assos Hotel.

Melinda shared his view. "There must be something better around here, maybe someplace with a pool."

"I can assure you that there are no other hotels, motels,

or inns in this part of the country," Elaine said with an angry flash of her crystal-green eyes as she pulled her long ginger hair into a ponytail. "We're lucky to find a bed under a roof. Need I remind you that we are not on holiday?"

Their accommodations at the gritty little hotel were simple: two hot and dusty rooms with twin beds, a toilet down a dimly lit, shabby hallway, no restaurant, no telephone, and no television. It was looking increasing bleak for Felix and Melinda.

In their room, Felix rummaged through his backpack, produced a book, and flopped onto his bed.

"Felix!" Melinda stormed. "We're here to find Joe and Harmony. We can't just sit around reading books."

Felix glared at his sister. "I happen to be reading the book Horace Stumpworthy wrote about Turkey."

"Horace Stumpworthy! As if he'd tell the world exactly where to look for the cave. He's the one who tried to prevent anyone from ever finding it! *And* he probably destroyed all the hairyglits anyway."

"Hieroglyphs," Felix corrected, with a condescending flip of the page.

"Whatever. If you recall, he even tried to get rid of Joe. I really doubt his book will help us locate anything." Melinda began pacing the tiny space between the two tiny beds. She pounded her fist into her other hand. "We've got to get out there and find them before it's too late."

Felix narrowed his eyes. "How are we supposed to find them when we have no idea where to look? If you haven't noticed, it's a big desert out there," he grumbled, waving a hand toward the cracked window.

Melinda ignored him. "I have an idea. The owner of this place said we could use his old motorbike."

"You mean that old rusty *moped* we saw when we drove up?" Felix's lips curled in disgust.

"That's the one. Mom and Dad even said that we should take him up on the offer."

Felix was skeptical, but he knew he had only two options: either give in or have to listen to her nagging for the rest of the day. "I suppose it would be okay," he mumbled. "You could always change into something if there's a problem." Melinda's eyes lit up at the suggestion. "I said *if there's a problem*," Felix repeated.

Minutes later, having secured the key from the hotel's owner, Felix kicked down on the starter of the ancient and rusty machine. Nothing happened. Again he kicked down on the starter, this time with more force, but still the moped was silent. Beads of sweat dribbled down his face. He looked up at Melinda, and shrugged. "If I can even get this piece of junk started," he huffed, "where should we go?"

Melinda rolled her eyes. "To find Joe and Harmony."

Felix didn't argue; it wouldn't do any good. He knew their search would be futile. The hills had a lot of caves in them, and without a map it was virtually impossible that they'd find the one Joe had talked about—but as far as Felix was concerned, anything that might shut his sister up was worth pursuing.

He pushed six more times on the starter. Finally there was a rumble beneath him, followed by a puff of gray smoke announcing that the engine had reluctantly come to life. Exhausted by the ordeal, Felix sat down and then pulled a pair of perfectly round, incredibly dark bug-eyed goggles over his glasses. Melinda squeezed onto the remaining sliver of seat behind him. Felix cranked up the throttle. The engine groaned and sputtered, a huge cloud of dark smoke burst into the air, and the bike jumped forward. Slowly and unsteadily, they chugged out of the village.

They hadn't been driving long when Melinda pounded on Felix's shoulders, screeching to be heard over the clanking motor. "My bum hurts," she cried as they skidded to a stop, causing a minor dust storm that billowed around them. She hopped off the bike with a sour look on her face.

"Come on, Melinda—this was your idea. If you're going to want to stop every two minutes…" Felix prattled on, but Melinda had become distracted by a bird flying directly above them and was deaf to her brother's complaints.

She closed her eyes and stood up, holding perfectly still. The only thing on her mind was the memory of feathers and flight, and within seconds she had transformed into a kestrel, flapping out of her clothes and disappearing into the sky.

"Melinda!" Felix yelled, but she didn't stop. "She is such a pain! I should just leave her to get shot and roasted for someone's dinner," he growled, hurriedly picking up her clothes and then climbing back onto the moped. "Idiot!" he screamed after her as he cranked up the accelerator, and the moped sped off again in all its sputtering glory.

Melinda was flying a bizarre pattern, swerving, diving, and looping the loop. She might look like a perfect kestrel, but she didn't fly like one. Felix tried to follow but her mad flight was difficult to keep up with. After a few minutes she leveled and took off, flying swiftly toward the hills.

An irresistible pull tugged her forward as mysterious instincts took command of her flight. She swept through the air on a mission to find her friends, whom she felt certain were somewhere nearby. Her excitement built with each flap of her wings. A certainty washed over her as her eyes fixed on a man in the distance. Her heart raced as she sped through the cloudless sky; her instincts exploded with the certainty that she had found Joe. Only the man on the hillside wasn't Joe.

The man, noticing the shadow that was now circling above him, looked up with a gaze that seemed to meet hers. Just as quickly he looked away, pulled his cap low over his face, gathered his tools, and walked to a small truck idling a few meters away. Without looking back at the hillside or Melinda he drove off, leaving a cloud of dust as his only legacy.

Melinda didn't follow. He wasn't as interesting as what he'd left behind.

Felix clunked up the hillside when he saw that Melinda was circling. He reached a small plateau just as Melinda dove toward the ground, directly at the front wheel of the moped. Felix cranked the bike in the opposite direction and spun out of control. Choking dust swirled around them, and for a few panicked seconds Felix thought that he might have run over his only sister. As the air cleared, he was relieved to see that he hadn't—but when Melinda got to her feet, instantly transforming back into a girl and completely ignoring his well-being, his relief soured.

"What do you think you're doing? You almost got us both killed!" he shouted, only growing angrier when Melinda ignored him and ran over to a pile of rubble. "*Get your clothes on before somebody comes by!*" he exploded.

Melinda didn't seem to be listening. "There was a man here a little while ago. He was digging over here," she called, pointing to the small opening in the hillside.

"So?"

"There's a cave…Joe and Harmony might be in there," she panted.

"What makes you think it's this cave?" Felix demanded, unconvinced.

"I just think we should have a look."

"Don't be stupid. Caves are dangerous," he said as he cranked up the accelerator. "Before we do anything, we should go back for Mom and Dad. Besides, that opening is too small and we don't have any tools."

"Athenites don't need tools." Melinda smirked and began to transform. Felix's stomach lurched at what he considered a grotesque metamorphosis, having never enjoyed the sight of one species contorting into another. His sister melted and expanded; fur sprouted all over her body and she grew to several times her normal size. Her face distorted as her nose and mouth ballooned outward.

Felix looked away before her change was complete, waiting several seconds before squinting back at her.

When he did, his lids sprang open—his eyes filled with tears and his body shook with spastic hysterics, nearly knocking him off the bike. Melinda had morphed herself into a huge, hairy *thing*. She was about the size of a bear, and from the back might have been mistaken for one but for the floppy white bunny ears sprouting from the top of her giant mouse head, which, not surprisingly, featured Melinda's big blue eyes and freckled cheeks on either side of her long mouse nose. Felix staggered, trying to keep the moped upright. "What are you supposed to be this time, a mutant mouse?" Melinda hissed in response, sending Felix deeper into hysterical fits. "Oh, I see!" he wailed. "A mutant *mousecat*!"

Melinda frowned, grinding her teeth. *He thinks he's so smart…he doesn't even know how to transform into anything,* she thought irritably. She turned toward the hillside and threw herself into digging. With her huge shovel-sized paws, she feverishly pulled rocks and dirt away from the small opening, making it larger by the minute. As soon as it was big enough for her, she squeezed through and disappeared from view.

CHAPTER THREE

Being inside the earth, with its dark, cool dampness, musty smells, and haunting echoes, made Melinda feel strangely invigorated. She imagined that she was the perfect likeness of a grizzly bear, and she felt invulnerable. But there was something else tingling at the edge of her senses: her nose told her that Joe and Harmony had been here.

She plodded along the passage with surprising ease; the earthquake seemed to have damaged only the area close to the opening. A short distance inside, the tunnel forked. To the left was a narrow, damp crevice, and to the right an opening that was considerably wider, with a surprising amount of light illuminating the pathway. Joe and Harmony's scent was indistinguishable now, muddled with the smells of the caves. With nothing to guide her but light, Melinda chose the right fork. Debris from the earthquake was everywhere now; it was as if the whole roof had fallen in. Undaunted, she kept following the light, crawling over jagged rocks and squeezing through the shrinking passage.

The state of the tunnel was making it difficult to get through in her current form. *I need to change into something else*, Melinda decided, freezing her movements and focusing on the memory of a gray shaggy dog. At once she shrank in size, her fur turned a steely gray, and her body changed from its bulky strength into the sleek form of a dog. *Piece of cake*, she thought as she pulled herself over the rubble and easily wiggled through the damaged passage.

The light was brighter the farther she went, and the sweet smell of fresh air intensified. She crouched low, feeling the stone of the passage rub against her back and belly as she pulled herself toward the cave opening, when suddenly the passage gave way, sending her sliding down a pile of rubble toward the cool brightness. But it wasn't sunlight she tumbled out into.

Instead, Melinda landed in a remarkable chamber where the air was sweet, not musty, and the light was incredibly bright, reflecting a rainbow of colors from walls that were anything but bland cave gray. Each wall was covered in intricate artwork, and the ceiling sparkled with hundreds of tiny lights that glistened through the rock.

The scene was dazzling. It was like an art gallery, and every centimeter of the walls was covered with pictures—beautiful images and symbols that told a story about an ancient civilization. The light and ventilation were delivered by hundreds of tiny tunnels carefully chiseled through the rock ceiling, letting both sunlight and fresh air into the compartment. Someone had obviously gone to a lot of trouble to make this place as comfortable as it was magnificent.

Hairyglits, Melinda thought excitedly as she admired the painted figures. There were pictures of prehistoric beasts, herds of antlered animals, serpents and frightening-looking flying creatures. There were panels of intricately carved symbols telling stories that Melinda couldn't understand. There were pictures of villages with men, women, children, and something Melinda found especially exciting: there were people pictured who had hooves and antlers and lions' heads and tails! Farther along, other drawings caught her eye, and she gasped in delight. There was a man becoming a bear, a woman changing into a tiger, and a child transforming into something akin to a dolphin. Without question these pictures identified the accepted existence of Athenites.

Melinda could barely contain her excitement. She had to go back for Felix; he had to see this unbelievable place. She turned to leave, but then stopped abruptly when she noticed a small wooden casket resting in the shadow of the wall.

Felix had remained at the entrance, calling to Melinda every few minutes. But she didn't yell, growl, or bark back. There were no sounds from inside the cave. "I've got to go in after her," he muttered as he paced. Then, talking himself out of it: "I can't, I don't have a torch. But I'm an Athenite—why don't I just transform and go find her?" A shiver ran up his back at the thought. "Because it's gross."

His watch told him he had been waiting for over an hour. It was a long time without any sound other than the scrunching of gravel under his feet. He had just sat down on a large rock near the opening, resting his head in his hands, when the rumble of falling rocks set his heart racing.

"Melinda! Are you okay?" His voice was shrill. More tumbling rocks made him jump to his feet. He was certain now that the sound wasn't coming from inside the cave.

His breathing quickened with the certainty that someone was coming up behind him. "Melinda," he croaked weakly. But Melinda didn't answer. Paralyzed, he remembered the man Melinda had seen earlier. *How am I going to explain that my sister is in the cave,* he thought helplessly, *and that she's actually this weird bear?* He spun around to face the presence at his back. No one was there.

His face glistened with sweat that soaked through his clothing. His whole body trembled. He turned back to the cave, wishing he could transform like his sister—but it was too late to learn that skill now. Again he felt someone creeping up behind him, and again he jerked around. No one. The sense that he wasn't alone consumed him, but he didn't know why. The only sound was the distant caw of a bird. He leaned into the cave again and squeaked for Melinda. Then fear consumed his very soul as he was grabbed from behind, a hand firmly clasped over his mouth.

Felix felt as if all the bones had been removed from his legs. He slumped to his knees. His thoughts floated away, down a long, dark tunnel where sound echoed before being absorbed by emptiness. He could barely feel the grip of his assailant as one by one he lost his senses. Then the sting of his face being slapped broke the darkness. Felix gasped and coughed and squinted against the blinding sunlight, staring into the blurred face of a woman.

"Harmony," he whispered hopefully, but as soon as his eyes regained their focus he realized he had guessed wrong. Dr. Harmony Melpot's tall, straight posture, perfectly styled short blond hair, strong, angular features, and healthy glow sometimes made her look a little too perfect, more like a statue than a real person. This woman didn't fit the same description. Her thin face was excessively gaunt, her sallow skin was covered in a layer of dirt, and the stench surrounding her would bring a fly back to life. Felix pushed away from her violently, scuttling backward in crab fashion.

"Will you *p-l-e-a-s-e* relax," the woman wheezed, her putrid breath spewing into his face.

Felix retched, still struggling against her grip as she pulled him into a thicket of shrubs and forced her filthy hand over his mouth. He bit her.

"What'd you do that for?!" she yelped. "Okay, I won't cover your mouth if you will *just keep quiet*."

Felix was about to make a run for it when a squeaking sound drew his attention. Through a tangle of branches he saw that a man was pushing the old moped toward them.

"I thought I'd better get this out of the way," the familiar voice announced. "Felix, it's good to see you. Something told me you and your family would be coming before too long." Joe Whiltshire propped the moped against a boulder, then covered it with a few branches. "That should camouflage it a little, just in case."

Felix took in the strong, handsome visage of Joe Whiltshire. He hadn't changed one iota since Felix had last seen him in Paris—he still had the look of a great explorer. He was even clean. Felix craned his neck back to stare again at the woman. "You really are Harmony," he wheezed, studying her in awe. Baffled, he turned to Joe. "I don't get it, if you look normal, then why does she look so bad?"

"Thanks a lot," Harmony snarled. "There aren't any showers in there, you know."

"I'm an Athenite," Joe answered matter-of-factly.

"So am I," Harmony sniveled. "Well, at least half of me is."

"True, but I can transform. In the old days, Athenites often survived when humans couldn't. Transformation allows us to exist in the environment where we find ourselves. It's nature's way." He smiled with a shrug. "When we were trapped in that cave I spent my days in various animal forms, adapting to the surroundings. It's amazing what some of the lower life forms can subsist on: grubs, worms, lichen, dirt." Felix winced at the thought. "Don't worry, I'm not planning to add these to my regular diet," Joe continued, "but you know, dirt is fine dining to an earthworm. Harmony wasn't too keen to adjust her diet, so she went without."

Felix grimaced, looking hard at Harmony. "You mean that you didn't eat all this time?"

"I wasn't going to eat bugs and worms—and sorry, Joe, no matter what you say, dirt isn't a treat. So I had to sleep instead. I can't become an animal, but I can use their strengths, like hibernation to conserve energy. Joe had to find a way out, and when he did he woke me up and here we are."

Felix's mouth dropped open. "No way, you didn't eat anything?"

Harmony groaned. "Let's *not* talk about food right now. I'm starving…literally."

"How did you get out? I didn't see you come through the entrance," Felix said.

"This cave is at least fifteen stories deep. There were a lot of entrances, but they were blocked. I finally found one that I could make big enough to crawl through. I'll fill you in on the details later, but right now I'm more interested in getting out of here." Joe looked up, jerking his head from side to side. "I thought Melinda and your parents would be with you."

Felix opened his mouth to explain when a thunderous eruption shook the rocks all around them. "What's happening?" he screamed over the sounds of the groaning earth.

Nobody answered. They didn't need to. The entire hillside shuddered, rocking them off their feet and toppling the moped over. "Earthquake!" Joe and Harmony yelled.

Felix ran toward the cave entrance. "Melinda is in the cave!"

"Felix, you stay with Harmony!" Joe shouted, pushing Felix back as he ran for the cave himself, stripping the shirt off his shoulders and transforming as he did, and then vanishing inside the crumbling opening.

Everything was quiet again and Felix and Harmony took deep breaths. The silence didn't last. Another shock vibrated the ground with twice the force as the first.

Harmony rested a hand on Felix's shoulder. "Joe and Melinda will be fine, even if the earthquake…" Her sentence was broken as a tremendous blast thundered beneath them. "That's not an earthquake!" Harmony yelled. "It's an explosion, and it sounds like the whole mountain is going to blow apart!"

"My sister is in there!" Felix cried. His eyes filled with terror as he ran for the cave. Harmony lunged, grabbing him before he could go in.

"Felix, no! You can't risk it! Joe will find her. He has to…"

"Melinda!" Felix howled. But all he heard was the boom of another explosion, and the crash of the cave crumbling in.

CHAPTER FOUR

Joe loped through the passage in the form of a lynx. Dust was clouding everything—he couldn't see, he couldn't hear, his sense of smell couldn't sift through the floating particles of dirt and rock to give him even a hint of where to find Melinda. He had no choice but to trust his instincts. Just as he had been sure of the Huttons' arrival in Turkey, Joe was sure he could find her.

The ground continued to shake. The normal sounds inside the cave were replaced with deafening, explosive echoes. Joe could smell smoke in the distance. The temperature was rising. He knew time was running out.

Never slowing, he raced along the passage toward a brilliant light that suggested another way out of the cave. He bounded over a pile of rubble and slid out of the tunnel into a brightly lit room. Blinded by the light reflecting off the dust-filled air, he couldn't see the shaggy gray dog lying at the base of the far wall.

Harmony held tightly to Felix's arm, preventing him from running into the cave. They stared helplessly as the

entrance vanished in a shower of rock and dirt. "NO!"
Felix cried, tearing out of Harmony's grasp, but it was too
late to run inside. He dropped to his knees and frantically
clawed at the earth.

"Felix! They'll get out through one of the other
entrances." Harmony tried, in vain, to pull him away from
the rubble.

The sound of distant explosions was so intense that
Harmony didn't even hear the vehicle driving up behind them.

The bright pink paint on the 1970 Cadillac was barely
recognizable through a thick covering of brown grime.
It had been caught in the rain of dirt and rocks from
the mountain demolition—extremely bad luck for its
passengers, since it was a convertible and they too were
covered in a heavy layer of dust. It skidded to a halt on the
plateau behind Felix and Harmony. The doors flew open
and both driver and passenger leapt out.

"Felix!" Jake and Elaine yelled at once.

Harmony jerked round. "Jake! Elaine! How did you
find us?"

"I flew a reconnaissance mission, then we borrowed
the innkeeper's car…but never mind about that right now.
Are you okay? We heard the explosions. Where's Melinda?"
Jake shouted over the rumbling.

With tears streaming down his cheeks, Felix panted,
"In the cave. She's trapped in the cave with Joe."

Elaine's face lost all color as she looked from Felix back
to Harmony. "Is there another entrance? We've got to
hurry and rescue them. Whoever is blasting this mountain
apart has already succeeded in destroying the other side.
There's nothing left over there."

Harmony stumbled back, her eyes wide. Determination
hardened her expression.

"We only have one option. Everyone, *dig*!"

Joe was just about to leave the chamber when he heard the bark behind him. He whirled around to find a gray dog getting to its feet. He couldn't understand what she was trying to say, since he was a different species, but he knew the dog must be Melinda. In the next second she was at his side, holding something tightly in her mouth. Together they bolted out of the chamber and dashed down the tunnel toward the entrance—but when they arrived, the opening was blocked.

An eerie silence settled over them. The respite from the explosions allowed them to hear the subtle sound of scratching from the other side. Immediately Melinda and Joe joined in the chorus of scraping. Soon a small section of the rubble broke open, letting in the sweet smell of fresh air. Seconds later it was big enough for a paw to push out. In a couple of minutes the hole was big enough for Melinda to squeeze through, helped by Felix pulling mightily from the other side. Joe scrambled out immediately behind her, grunting as he fought his way through the opening.

Relief soothed everyone, except Harmony, who whipped her head around to regard them all. "Run! Get away from the cave—now!"

She didn't need to shriek twice. Everyone bolted, running as fast as they could away from the cave while the ground beneath their feet first shimmied and then quaked violently. They had barely made it to safety when a powerful tremor shook the earth, sending them toppling and rolling down the hillside. What followed was an explosion of colossal magnitude. The deafening sound of rock collapsing against rock, along with a dense curtain of earth and sand discharged into the air, was unbelievable.

Enshrouded in the billowing cloud of dust, they had to

rely on shouts and cries to locate each other. When things settled, there was no mistaking the devastation. The cave had totally collapsed. Melinda burst into tears. Had she been two seconds slower in her escape, she would be dead, crushed under tons of rock.

Everyone was covered in a thick layer of grit, making the two-hour drive back to Assos very unpleasant. Melinda spent the entire journey in complete silence. Felix, his arm around her shoulders, spent the time really missing those annoying things she usually did.

The Cadillac hardly resembled its former glory. Not only was it coated in dirt, it looked like a family of sheep had tap danced on its hood and trunk. The moped (which was no prize to begin with) had fared only slightly better. Joe had to use his winning smile and all his diplomatic charm to explain to the owner what had happened. That and a sizeable handful of cash calmed him only slightly, but he did agree not to call the police just yet.

Now, crowded into Jake and Elaine's tiny room preparing for their departure (at the request of the innkeeper), they all tried to make sense of what had *and was* happening.

Melinda told everyone about the fantastic cave art and ancient writing in the chamber. She told them about the small wooden box and showed them what she had found inside: four leather-bound books that she'd been able to carry out. Each was about the size of a diary, and the pages were a maze of intricate and colorful hieroglyphs. After flipping through each one, she looked up sadly. "They don't have any of the drawings from the walls—the pictures of the Athenites living with humans."

Joe looked enviously at Melinda. "I wish I could've

seen those walls…they sound even more fantastic than the ones I saw all those years ago." He paused, examining a page of the journal. "This language isn't the same as in the other caves. The symbols might be telling the same story. They are very similar, but I can't translate them."

"Let me have a look." Elaine examined a few pages in each book. "It's not a language I'm familiar with, but my work in ancient languages was always a little weak."

"Don't look at me," Jake shrugged. "I know a little Latin, but nothing about hieroglyphs."

"I'm afraid I'm in the same boat. What about James Mulligan? He teaches ancient languages," Harmony suggested.

Felix was looking through another of the journals. "I'm sure I saw some books with this kind of writing in Horace Stumpworthy's library in Paris." He looked from Joe to Harmony, both of whom had known Stumpworthy very well in the past.

"He *was* an expert in languages, modern and ancient, but he's no longer in a position to help." Harmony sighed. "And to tell you the truth neither am I. I'm starving. If you'll excuse me, I'm just going to grab something to eat."

"Harmony, I know you're used to the new you…*hey*, so am I! But you might just want to clean up a little first," Joe reminded her.

"Oh, right." Harmony smiled thinly. "I guess I'm getting a little too used to living as a cavewoman."

In Melinda's mind she saw clearly the painted walls of the chamber. Its destruction didn't make any sense. "Why would someone blow up the cave?"

"I don't know, but I do know we shouldn't stick around to find out," said Joe. "We're out of luck for tonight, but I think we should get on the first flight out of here tomorrow."

"Where will we go?" Melinda asked, even though she had an inkling what his answer would be.

A wry smile curled the corners of Joe's mouth. "We need to be in a place where we have ample resources at hand. Felix made an excellent observation a minute ago. Why don't we use the hospitality and resources of our good friend Horace Stumpworthy?"

CHAPTER FIVE

It was an image that continued to haunt Felix: Professor Horace Stumpworthy's expression, a mixture of terror and amazement, as he felt the pierce of the needle. Eyes filled with contempt, he watched helplessly as Felix removed the hypodermic syringe now emptied of the powerful Burungo sedative. The professor didn't look so distinguished now as he slumped onto the floor. Then Joe administered the wolfbane, forcing Stumpworthy's transformation into a small, white, helpless lemming. The image was firmly etched in Felix's mind, a memory he dearly wished he didn't possess.

Stumpworthy had tried to destroy the Huttons with a rare and horrific virus—a strain so powerful as to kill a human or force an Athenite into involuntary transformation. Joe Whiltshire had suffered for years, trapped in the body of Aesop, Melinda's pet rabbit, all because of Stumpworthy's selfish cruelty. Even Harmony and the dithering old Professor James Mulligan had almost become his victims.

Still, Felix didn't feel good about the part he'd played in destroying a man who had once been his hero. How could anyone enjoy the destruction of another? Maybe in the movies, but this was real life. For the last few months, Felix had pushed the images aside, letting the memory wither in the back of his mind. But arriving at Professor Horace Stumpworthy's Paris estate brought them to life again.

Jake seemed to sense his son's anxiety as the taxi pulled in through the imposing black iron gates, carrying them up the long driveway that led to the front of the house. "It's okay, Felix. I think I know how you must feel coming back here. I don't think any of us are excited about returning, but it is the best option."

"Look on the bright side," Melinda announced. "You get to spend some time with Old Walrus Face."

"Melinda!" Elaine scolded. "I told you not to call him that. Professor James Mulligan is a brilliant man, as well as a good friend."

"I agree with your mother," Jake added seriously, "you must be respectful. After all, the poor man can't help the fact that he looks just like a fat old walrus."

Stumpworthy's palatial home was as imposing as ever. Nothing seemed to have changed—the lush gardens that surrounded the house had been meticulously attended, the twelve marble steps leading up to the front door still hosted huge urns of magnificent white flowers, and the bougainvillea that crawled up the front of the classic French gray stone mansion were still bursting with an abundance of pink and purple blossoms. No one could have guessed that the famous professor was no longer king of his castle.

Not unless they were invited inside.

James Mulligan, disheveled as usual, opened the door on the first knock. "I see you've all made it," he greeted them warmly. "Please come inside. I was a bit surprised to receive your phone call from Istanbul. I'm eager to hear more about what has been happening."

"It looks like a scene from *Great Expectations*," Melinda quipped as she stepped into the formal two-story foyer. Dust layered the furnishings, cobwebs hung on the statues and paintings like tinsel, and dust bunnies roamed free, darting under furniture and dancing elegantly across the floor in the breezes through the open door.

"What happened to this place? Where are the servants?" wheezed Felix as he ran a finger through the thick layer of dust that entombed the ten-foot-tall, lion-headed statue of the god Bes that stood in the centre of the room.

"They've all gone, I'm afraid," James Mulligan explained. "There was nothing for it. I can barely pay the electricity bills for this place, let alone pay servants' salaries. Let's go down to the library; it's the only room I use now. Sad, really—this house used to have such life."

Everyone followed Mulligan as he plodded down the darkened hallway and into the library. The room had that unmistakable "lived-in" décor, with an assortment of used cups and glasses, a partially eaten sandwich, and various newspapers strewn around. "Sorry about the mess," the professor grimaced, "I've been too busy to get to the cleaning, what with working at the Science School."

Harmony cringed, feeling protective and a little guilty about the school where she had worked as a teacher for many years. "How are things at the school? Everything was running smoothly when I left for Turkey. You haven't had any problems, I hope?"

"No, no problems…everything is running as smoothly as can be expected," Mulligan pepped.

"*As can be expected?*" Harmony repeated anxiously.

"My dear, the school is the same as when you left it. Don't let my housekeeping put you off—I'm a much better school administrator than I am a maid." He plopped into his favorite overstuffed chair next to the impressively large fireplace, motioning for his guests to make themselves comfortable on the numerous sapphire-blue, silk-embroidered sofas. "I'm glad to see that you're back safe and sound," Mulligan continued. "You might want to settle into your old rooms you'll find they're just as you left them." He smiled warmly.

"I'm eager to get a look at these books you've found. Mind if I do that while you settle in?"

Upstairs, Melinda found Mulligan had been true to his word; nothing had changed in her room. The massive four-poster bed had not been made since she had crawled out from under the covers several months before, and the long, pink, floral curtains were still drawn over the floor-to-ceiling windows, eliminating any hint of the natural light that usually brightened and warmed the room. Even the unfinished drawing of her former rabbit Aesop lay undisturbed on the writing table. Felix walked in behind her. "Mine's the same, but at least I made my bed before we left."

"I left it for the maid! From the looks of things, Mulligan must've sacked the whole staff the day we left."

Felix nodded. "I know Mulligan is a wonderful teacher, but he's a bit of a waste on the home front, isn't he?" Felix flopped onto the bed, causing a minor dust storm. "Gross!" he squealed, jumping up again. "We'd better get downstairs, there's no telling what he'll do with those books you found in the cave."

As they made their way along the hallway, they noticed that the addition of copious amounts of dust was not the only change to the house. The once bright and welcoming passageway, with its shiny white marble floors partially covered with richly exotic and colorful rugs, now looked dull, dusty, dark, and uninviting. Absent also were the fresh flowers that had lent their fragrance to every room.

"I hate to say it, but I liked the place better when Stumpworthy was around," Felix sighed.

Melinda smiled. "*Felix...*he's still here."

"I know that, but you know what I mean. It's just not the

same." Down the hallway, the welcoming warmth from the library beckoned. Felix sighed. "When I arrived here last year to attend Stumpworthy's Science School, I spent all my time in the library."

"You always spend all your time in a library."

"Yeah, but this was different. Since I wasn't exactly thrilled about being an Athenite, it freaked me out to see the professor's collection of artwork." He pointed to a statue of Pegasus, the mythological winged horse, then at a painting of a boy with horns and goat's hooves playing a flute. "Every room in this house is loaded with half-animal, half-human sculptures and paintings. They reminded me too much of my relatives. The Library is the only room that doesn't have any of them. It was my sanctuary."

"Do they still bug you?" Melinda asked.

"Not really. But I'll probably spend most of my time there anyway. Some of those cobwebs in the rest of the house are huge…I'm not looking forward to meeting the spider who designed them," he grimaced as they stepped into the library.

"Ah, Felix, Melinda…found your rooms okay?" Mulligan looked over his spectacles at them, not having budged from the big chair. "Melinda, these journals are incredible. What a tremendous find." He returned his attention to the book he had been examining, not waiting for a response from either of them.

Melinda bounded into the room and claimed the nearest sofa for her own, sprawling unceremoniously across its soft cushions.

Felix remained standing, now feeling very awkward to be back in the room that had once served as his refuge. As with everything in Horace's world, the room defied mediocrity. With its circular construction and three floors of splendid ornamentation, it was itself a work of art. The main floor provided a relaxed environment, with luxurious furnishings surrounding the enormous fireplace on one side and a quiet study with a large desk and four comfortable chairs on the other. The next two floors, accessible by a circular staircase, were like galleries that opened to the centre of the chamber, with low, ornately carved golden railings at their edge. Each floor had six tall windows, evenly spaced to capture the perfect amount of natural light no matter what time of year or what inclement weather might be expected. But as extraordinary as the room was in its design, the most amazing attribute was its collection of books. The outer walls of all three floors were lined with towering bookshelves that held thousands of volumes of books about every imaginable subject.

It was surreal for Felix to see his family and friends comfortably positioned around this room now—the room in which, not more than a year ago, Professor Horace Stumpworthy had tried to destroy them all.

Jake was on the first-floor gallery, examining volume after volume of ancient language references. On the ground floor, Joe was studying one of the precious journals while reclining on the sofa facing the fireplace. On the other end of the same sofa sat Harmony, untroubled by the activity around her, showing no interest in anything except a little snooze. Her head was cradled by the soft armrest, her eyes flickering almost imperceptibly under tightly closed lids.

Across the room, clicking away at the keys on her laptop, Elaine was working at Horace Stumpworthy's antique desk, the very desk at which Stumpworthy became the victim instead of the villain. Felix stared unblinking at the place where his mentor had sunk to his knees. A shiver ran up his spine, and Felix pushed the memory away as quickly as he had conjured it up. He flopped onto the sofa closest to the popping fire and turned to Mulligan. "Professor, can you translate the journals?"

"Not immediately…it's not a language I've studied before," Mulligan reflected seriously.

Joe looked up. "The grouping of the symbols doesn't

make sense. I hate to say it, but we could use Horace right now—he was a master at decoding. By the way, how is the little vermin?"

"Docile. I almost feel sorry for him. You might want to examine him, Jake," Mulligan called up to Jake, who was now on the second floor.

"Shouldn't waste your time," Joe snorted.

"Can I see him?" Melinda asked.

Elaine looked up from her computer. "Melinda, you may *see* him, but please don't try to make him into a pet."

Without lifting his bulky body out of the comfortable chair, Mulligan called to Jake, "I've kept him in the laboratory downstairs. You remember the way." Melinda darted out of the library with Jake close behind.

She trotted through the foyer, then down the stairs to the basement as if her last encounter with Stumpworthy's mansion had been yesterday instead of a year ago. Recessed floor lighting illuminated the stairway, but nonetheless, the passage seemed dull and uninviting. Jake followed at a slower, less enthusiastic pace.

When she reached the bottom step, Melinda gasped at what remained of the underground retreat. Dry, brown, skeletal plants were the only remnants of the exotic flowers that once grew in giant urns set around the pool. The pool itself was looking no better, its once clean, clear water now clouded with a greenish tinge.

"Not very inviting," Jake said as he joined Melinda on the step. "It looks like James hasn't kept up with the pool maintenance."

"That's no big surprise, when you look at the way he's taken care of the rest of the house," Melinda replied. "I doubt if he would ever go swimming anyway—he may look like a walrus but I doubt if he would be able to swim like one."

"It's a big house," Jake said, his tone gently scolding. "Taking care of everything is a full time job for an entire staff; one man couldn't possibly do it all."

Together they crossed to the back wall and passed through the doorway hidden in the mural and into the lab. Now it was Jake's turn to gasp. While the rest of the house looked starkly different from in its former glory, the laboratory had not changed a bit. The shiny floor and dust-free counters were just as they been before, and air still alive with the hum of expensive equipment and the smell of caustic chemicals.

"It looks exactly the same," Jake whispered.

Melinda looked up at her father, seeing the worried look on his face. "Mulligan must still use it."

Jake didn't move, staring straight ahead at a cage on the counter. He felt certain it was the same one that had imprisoned him.

Melinda followed his gaze, then walked over and touched the cold metal bars. Instantly her mind returned to the night when she'd found her father trapped in the body of a mouse, held prisoner in this very cage. It sent chills up her spine. The cage was still in use, it looked like: it had a food bowl containing bits of grain and carrots, as well as a half-full water bottle clipped to the side. Then the subtle movement of a small creature half hidden inside the paper shavings caused her stomach to tighten. She glanced backward at her father, then turned slowly back to watch the small white creature burrowing as far as it could under the shavings.

She unlatched the door and carefully reached inside. The instant her fingers touched the smooth fur of the animal, it kicked away into a corner of the cage. Now trapped, Melinda easily lifted it up by the scuff of its neck and pulled it out of the cage. The little white lemming struggled in vain as Melinda held it securely.

"Do you want to see him?" she asked her father.

Jake frowned and then reluctantly examined the little animal. "He seems fine," Jake said, not sounding particularly pleased about it. "Now put him back."

Melinda shook her head. "He's an animal now—he can't hurt us or anyone else. I think he needs to come upstairs for a while. It can't be very nice to be locked in a cage."

"It isn't," her father snapped.

Melinda nodded to herself. Then she reached back inside the cage and grabbed a carrot, bringing it to the squirming lemming's mouth as she and Jake left the lab behind.

CHAPTER SEVEN

The sounds in the library had returned to those of clicking computer keys, the crackling fire, and the soft whisper of pages being turned until Harmony suddenly snorted herself awake, looking up with a start. "Someone's here," she yawned.

Mulligan, head still angled toward the book on his lap, looked at her over his glasses. "We're all here, dear. You must have drifted off."

"No, James, not us. Someone else is here."

James Mulligan opened his mouth to refute her claim, but the only sound was the deafening gong announcing someone's arrival at the front door.

"Oh, bother! I keep forgetting about your Athenite senses…it's like living with Lassie. Excuse me a moment. I'll see who's at the door. Probably another delivery—I can't tell you how many I've had over the past couple of months. Books, paintings, sculptures…Horace didn't waste any time spending his money," Professor Mulligan grumbled to himself as he trundled to the door.

When he opened it to reveal a scruffy-looking man waiting on the front step, he wished he had sent one of the others to receive the visitor.

"May I help you?" he asked.

"Yes—well, I hope you can. My name is Augusto Chambers." The man waited expectantly, as if Mulligan was meant to recognize him, or at least his name.

Mulligan sized up what he thought as a rather rough example of humanity. The man's clothes were outdated, looking maybe ten years out of style—clean but shabby, with a few moth holes here and there. They didn't seem well fitted, perhaps originally made for someone considerably lighter in build. His hair was shaggy and gray, his face muscular, his expression serious, perhaps even harsh.

"I'm sorry, doesn't ring a bell…who are you hoping to find?" Mulligan asked with a tremor in his voice.

"I know Horace is…ah…let us just say *unavailable*. You must be Professor James Mulligan. Look, I know you have guests, but if I could just come in…"

Whoever this man was, he knew too much, and Mulligan didn't know what to do about it. "Yes, I think you had better come inside. I'll get…ah…Joe Whiltshire for you."

"Joe Whiltshire, back from the dead," the man said flatly.

"Wait here!" Mulligan yelped, quickly returning to the library. He was shaking, perspiration beading on his forehead. He didn't care whether Joe or anyone else handled this; he just knew it wasn't going to be him. "Joe, a Mr. Chambers in the foyer says he needs to talk to you," he announced as he scuttled into the library.

"Chambers?"

"Yes, ah, let's see…Arthur? No, no…Andrew?" Mulligan stuttered, finding it difficult to catch his breath.

"Augusto!" Joe didn't need to wait for Mulligan to get the name right as the man walked into the library. "What are you doing here?" Joe snarled.

"I might ask the same of you," Augusto Chambers sniped back.

"If you've come to see your buddy, he's indisposed. But I'll be sure to let him know you stopped by," Joe said tersely.

At that moment, Melinda bounded back into the room, clinging tightly to the little white lemming. "I tried to get him to eat a carrot but he wouldn't!" She paused when she noticed the visitor. She smiled as if she knew him, looking directly into his eyes. "You're Oscar, aren't you?" she asked excitedly.

Everyone looked between Melinda and the fidgeting white lemming, and then Augusto Chambers. Melinda continued to hold Chambers's gaze.

"Melinda, what are you talking about?" Elaine asked.

Melinda shook her head. "He's Oscar, Mom. Don't you remember that dog that used to hang out around here? Felix, you must remember him—you were here longer than any of us."

Felix glared at his sister. He remembered the sickly looking, shaggy gray dog named Oscar, but this obviously wasn't him. "Don't be stupid," he barked nervously. "This is a *man*, if you haven't noticed, and his name isn't Oscar!"

Elaine looked awkwardly at their visitor. "Mr. Chambers, I must apologize. My daughter has a very active imagination."

"It's all right, everyone. Chambers knows all about Athenites. Don't you, Augusto?" Joe chided.

Chambers didn't take his eyes off of Melinda. "How did you know about me…about Oscar?"

"I recognized you." Melinda shrugged, stroking the little white lemming she held tightly.

Chambers smiled incredulously. "Well, young lady, you are correct. I went by the name of Oscar for years. Horace and I did a lot of work together; several years ago I suffered an accidental exposure to a virus we'd been developing. It forced my transformation into the body of a dog, and until recently that's how I remained. Now, however, I have returned to my former self. I am Augusto Chambers, and I am very pleased to meet you, Ch'ing-wa Sheng." He bowed formally to Melinda.

"Ch'ing-wa what?" Professor Mulligan asked.

"The Chinese frog fairy?" Felix and Melinda stuttered in unison. "Like from the stories Mom read us when we were little?" Melinda added.

Elaine left her keyboard and stood beside her daughter as she addressed the room. "Ch'ing-wa Sheng is a very important fairy in Chinese mythology. It represents a spirit who has vision and understanding. But what does it have to do with Melinda?"

"The ability to recognize Athenites was once nicknamed Ch'ing-wa Sheng—at least when I was a child. It's a very rare talent, you should be very proud," Augusto said, holding his stare.

Joe had at last lost patience with his unwelcome guest. He strode into the middle of the gathering, putting himself between Melinda and the stranger. "What's going on, Chambers? What do you want?" Joe demanded.

"Oh, not very much," Augusto assured him, his eyes idly scanning the library. "I just came to pick up a few things I left here all those years ago…a few books, some personal papers. Mind if I take a look around?" he asked with a warm smile that looked ill suited to his face.

"Actually, I do," Joe replied, crossing his arms. "We've only just arrived and we're all too tired for this sort of thing. Perhaps you should come back at another time."

"It really is very important that I find them," Augusto insisted. He stepped to the side, as if to go around Joe, but Joe mirrored him exactly, cutting him off from the rest of the library.

"Why don't you tell me specifically what you're looking for, and if we run across anything, I'll let you know," Joe spit out.

Augusto was silent for a moment, scrutinizing Joe with narrowed eyes. Then he seemed to make a decision of some kind; with a sigh, he took a step back and reached into his pocket, digging out a business card.

"Horace and I used a few books in our work—manuals, actually—that might come in handy for my next job. They all have my name inscribed on the title page. Call me if you find them." He handed his card to Joe and then turned away, pausing to smile down at the lemming in Melinda's hands. "I suffered for many years for our work," he said, so quietly Melinda was sure only she could hear him. "Perhaps now it is your turn, old friend." He reached out as if to pet the little creature—but the second he moved, the lemming went crazy in Melinda's hands, squirming so hard she could barely hold him. Melinda gasped as the furry rodent slipped through her palms, bringing her hands together in a sharp clap as the lemming took off across the library.

"Oh no!" she cried, watching the fuzzy white creature's body disappear under a table.

"Catch him—quick!" Joe ordered.

Everyone scrambled to obey. Melinda was on her knees at once, struggling to spot the tiny lemming. It led her on a merry chase across the floor of the enormous library, under tables and behind couches and through the legs of chairs until finally she caught up with it beneath Stumpworthy's enormous desk. Melinda lunged and wrapped her hands tightly around the little furball—but her shoulder knocked into the desk as she dove, and the impact shook a few things loose, pens and papers raining down above her. Something heavy struck her head and made her yelp. She didn't realize it was one of the journals until a hand reached down into her field of vision, gripping the journal at one dusty corner. Then she looked up and realized exactly who it was that had picked up the precious book.

Augusto didn't say anything. His eyes roved over the journal, devouring the pattern on the intricate cover; then he set it gently back on the desk and offered his hand to Melinda.

"He always was a troublesome one," Augusto murmured.

"All right, that's enough!" Joe stormed, striding across the room and snatching Augusto's arm. "You've far overstayed your welcome. I think you had better be on your way."

"Certainly," Chambers agreed, withdrawing his arm from Joe's grip. "Just give me a call if you find any of my things." Then he walked toward the door with Joe behind him, glancing back briefly at Melinda holding the squirming lemming.

Joe marched Augusto out to the main door and flung it open, his fingers stiff around the knob as the unwanted visitor made a leisurely exit. Augusto stopped on the front step and turned to face him once more.

"I know you harbor a lot of resentment toward me, Joe, but my work on the virus was a long time ago. Until this afternoon, I thought you were dead. I'm glad to find I was mistaken."

Joe didn't respond, just holding the door open to encourage him to leave.

Augusto smiled. "I know you will find this hard to believe, but I've changed a lot from when you knew me before. Goodbye, Joe—I doubt you will see me again." Then he turned away and walked slowly down the steps, hands shoved down in his pockets.

Joe closed the door firmly behind him, and then stood a few seconds just holding it shut, thinking. The hallway took on a strange echoing quality as he walked back to the library. He hadn't given Augusto Chambers a thought in years. Now his mind was flooded with memories

"Who was that guy?" Felix asked as soon as Joe came back into the room.

"Augusto Chambers was at university with Horace and me. I never really got on with him, but Horace was as close to him as he was to me. Maybe it was jealousy on my part, but I really resented Horace's friendship with the guy. I didn't trust him. I thought he was the odd man out…now

I know *I* was. Horace and Augusto shared the same hatred of humans, both bent on keeping the reality of Athenites a secret so that they would be able to satisfy their own greed. They used their transformation abilities to exploit human society, making at least Horace a very rich man. As you recall, the reason Stumpworthy wanted to eliminate all of us was because of our work attempting to provide enough factual information to take Athenites out of the storybooks and announce our existence to the real world."

"But maybe Oscar—I mean Augusto—was telling the truth. Living the life of a dog for so long was bound to change him," Melinda suggested.

"Sorry, kid, I don't buy that. Whatever Chambers is after is probably still here, and valuable in some way. He's not the sentimental type."

The lemming began squeaking and struggling to get free. "It's okay, it's okay," Melinda cooed.

"Melinda, he's not a real lemming—he's Stumpworthy. Put him back in his cage before he bites you or someone else," Felix insisted.

Melinda pouted only briefly. For when she looked at the face of the cute little lemming, she saw clearly the image of an angry Horace Stumpworthy staring back.

CHAPTER EIGHT

After a week in Paris, a new order had taken over the household. At precisely nine o'clock every morning, everyone gathered in the library to discuss the decoding of the Turkish journals. The process of decrypting the mysterious hieroglyphs was dominating life for everyone, except for Melinda, who found it a tedious bore.

"I'll wait for the movie," she quipped one day, stomping out of the library and waiting just outside the door for at least one person to beg her to stay and express their opinion that her contribution was crucial to the effort. But no one did. Days passed without so much as a simple query as to why she was no longer a member of the library brigade.

When it was painfully obvious that she was not needed, or even missed, Melinda decided to find her own space, finally taking sanctuary in the conservatory at the far end of the house.

As with the rest of the mansion, the room had seen better times. The one-time award-winning orangery now stood in decay. The hundreds of plants were brown-brittle skeletons of what had once been exotic tropical specimens. Only the cacti were unscathed by the drought that had decimated the once beautiful space. Water spots and muddy smudges obscured the tall windows that looked out across the back gardens, once accessible through exquisite glass doors that led out onto a stone terrace. Rust had eroded their ornate metal frames, and the beveled glass panes were so dirty it was difficult to see clearly through them. It seemed to Melinda that those doors had been locked for a very long time, and the key was nowhere in sight.

Even given its dilapidated state, Melinda was not dissuaded. She watered and nurtured the plants. She swept and tidied up the dusty remnants of dead vegetation. She even tried her best to clean the windows, turning all those dirty splotches into watered-down, milky-brown streaks.

Most of her efforts paid off. After only a few days, green shoots appeared in the planters holding the heartier species. Others, having long ago given up on life, were relegated to the compost bucket she kept by the permanently locked doors.

Another day dawned and life got underway as the clock chimed nine. The procession of decoders headed for the library as Melinda skipped toward the conservatory. It was just like all the days that preceded it, but for one strange alteration—as Melinda rounded the final corner in the hallway on her last leg of her journey, three brown leaves danced toward her along the marble floor. No sooner had they tumbled past when a deep russet-colored leaf skittered into her foot. As she bent down to pick up the wayward foliage, several more specimens swept across the floor past her. The breeze that brushed across her face answered the question as to what was making the leaves move, but that left an even bigger question. There were no open windows or doors in this part of the house.

She squinted at the glass doors that led from the hallway into the conservatory—doors that she was convinced she had closed the day before but that now stood open. Creeping stealthily along the passageway to the sound of her own heartbeat thumping in her ears, she entered the conservatory. Inside, the breeze was beyond brisk, a downright zephyr. The locked doors that led out into the garden were flung wide open.

With a dizzying pivot, Melinda spun around and darted back down the passageway. As she rounded the corner that led to the library she collided with someone with such force that she was knocked off her feet, landing painfully on her bum.

Jake Hutton, stunned by the impact from his daughter, looked troubled. "What are you doing tearing around the hallway like that?"

She hoisted herself back to her feet and yelled, "The locked doors are open!"

Jake looked at his daughter and nodded sullenly. "That makes sense," he stated.

"No, it doesn't, because there isn't a key," she rattled.

Jake frowned. "There obviously is a key, and somebody has used it." He paused, stroking his chin.

"But who? I've been looking for days. I had asked everyone and they all said they hadn't seen it."

Jake raised a single brow. "A lot of other people had access to this house before we arrived."

Melinda clapped her hands against her cheeks and gasped, "Maybe someone came back to steal something."

"Perhaps." Jake nodded. "I was just downstairs to make sure that our little rodent friend had enough food and water. Only he wasn't there…both he and his cage are gone."

"Augusto!" Joe sneered, appearing unexpectedly behind them. "Sorry, I didn't mean to startle you, but I had a feeling that something was happening down here. I came to investigate."

"You heard something," Jake nodded hopefully.

"No, I didn't hear anything…it was just a strange sense that something wasn't right." Joe snorted. "Anyway, I would imagine that Augusto has returned to collect *his things*, as he put it. Probably wanted a little revenge on his old friend." He took a couple of steps toward the conservatory. "Let's check that nothing else has been disturbed. It might also be a good idea to see that all the locks are changed. As for our dear Horace, I say good riddance to the little furball."

Melinda turned the shiny new gold key until the lock clicked, then pushed the double glass doors open. The unusual happenings of the morning had helped her greatly. It turned out the only thing that had gone missing was Stumpworthy, and his well-being proved to be of little concern to the rest of the household. But the benefit to Melinda didn't come from his bad fortune. It came from the flurry of activity that took place afterward. Every lock and key in the mansion had been changed, and now Melinda was in possession of the key that would open her conservatory to the great gardens beyond.

She pranced out onto the stone terrace, jumping and spinning and humming to herself. Around and around she waltzed and sang, stopping abruptly when she heard clapping coming from the conservatory.

"Bravo!" Harmony cheered from the doorway. "It looks like you're celebrating something." She smiled. "I actually thought you might be upset with Horace's disappearance— he was cute as a lemming."

Melinda shrugged. "I would have felt badly if he had been a real lemming, but since he's not, I don't care what happens to him. Even so, that's not why I'm celebrating."

Harmony raised an eyebrow. "Oh? Then what is causing such jubilation out here?"

With her arms spread out at her sides, Melinda spun a circle. "I just like being outside."

Harmony stepped onto the terrace, looking out across

the garden and then back to Melinda "What was that tune you were humming? It sounded very familiar, but for some reason I can't place it."

Melinda wrinkled her nose. "I don't think it has a name. It's just the music from here."

"From here?" Harmony folded her arms and looked questioningly at Melinda. "I didn't realize Horace had his own symphony."

"I suppose you could call it *his* music, since this was his house." Melinda nodded thoughtfully as she shuffled over to the steps that led down to the lawn. She plopped onto the top step, turning to look at Harmony over her shoulder. "Can I ask you something?" Harmony nodded. Melinda looked out across the garden before continuing, "Do you ever wish you could transform?"

Harmony smiled kindly as she sat down next to Melinda. "Sure…at least, I did when I was your age. It was difficult being only one-half Athenite. You remember that my mother was Joe's sister and my dad was human?" Melinda nodded. "When I was younger, I remember longing to fly— what a thrill that must be. But as I got older I learnt to appreciate the talents I did possess. In some ways I think I'm very lucky, because I don't have to transform to use animal strengths at any time. My eyes can focus in the dark like a cat's, I can sniff out things like a bloodhound, I can even run pretty darn fast, if I do say so myself."

"That's so cool. I like transforming, but I wish I could do things like you."

Harmony laughed. "That's what my mom had always said. I know for a fact that she wished she had my hearing. I remember when I was a teenager…all those sleepovers, dances, parties! I'll bet Mom wished she could hear what we were really up to."

"Where are your parents now?" Melinda asked.

Harmony sighed. "They died in an accident about twelve years ago. I miss them, and I try to remember that through my memories they're still with me. They taught me a lot in the time we had together, like the concept that life is all related, all connected."

"Is that why you're named Harmony, because of the harmony of life?"

Harmony chuckled. "Actually, no, but that would have made sense. I was named after *He Aeros Musike*: music of the air. My mother used to tell me this story about how all places had their own special music, and that if you were in tune with your surroundings you could hear it."

"That's so funny!" Melinda's eyes sparkled. "That's what we were just talking about."

"Sorry?" Harmony rocked backward.

Melinda laughed loudly, jabbing Harmony in the arm with her finger. "You know…like what you called Stumpworthy's symphony."

Harmony stared intently at Melinda. "I don't understand."

"The music in the air." Melinda rolled her eyes. "The melody I was humming a few minutes ago…the music that belongs to this place. Every place has its own sound," Melinda tried to explain, but it was painfully obvious that Harmony didn't hear anything, and perhaps did not even believe her.

CHAPTER NINE

Felix had ignored the activity surrounding the break-in, choosing to continue working on the translations of the hieroglyphs. While not an expert, he had always received top marks in Latin and etymology, a course that gave him a basic understanding of languages. He had taught himself to read hieroglyphs a few years earlier and had written an entire essay for history class using the exotic symbols of ancient Egypt.

The sun had shed its last rays of the day at least two hours before he looked up from his work. "This is nuts. How am I going to sort through this stuff? Mulligan's an expert, and he's clueless. I doubt if even Stumpworthy could decipher these things." Frustrated but not discouraged, he carried on.

By nine o'clock that night, with his glasses resting near the tip of his nose, Felix was still grinding through the journals. "I don't get it." He sighed, disappointed. "Right when I think I'm onto something…it all changes," he announced to Professor Mulligan, who was snoring rhythmically from his chair in front of the fire. Felix dropped his head back against his chair, causing his glasses to slide back into their proper place at the bridge of his nose. He looked over at the snoozing professor and sighed. "I've been sitting here all day, and I haven't gotten anywhere!"

Mulligan cracked his eyes open. "I'm sorry, Felix, what was that?"

Felix looked down at his work, shaking his head. "I've tried everything, even the methods used to decode the Rosetta Stone, but nothing works—not all the time, anyway. I've been able to translate words, but when I put them together they don't make sense."

He looked back at Mulligan, but the professor was sputtering and grunting his way back to sleep.

"What's the point?" Felix stood up stiffly, massaged his legs, and then stretched. "Tomorrow is another day."

"Melinda, it's getting late," Harmony yawned. "We've been at this for hours and I can't hear any music."

"You must be able to." Melinda clicked her tongue. "When I was humming the music on the terrace, you said it sounded familiar."

"Lots of music sounds familiar…the tune you were singing probably sounds like something else I've heard." Harmony noted the disappointment in Melinda's expression. "Look, I appreciate you sharing your ideas with me, and I've enjoyed spending a lovely time in your conservatory with you, but I simply cannot hear music in the air." She took a couple of steps toward the door and then stopped. "Maybe the problem is that I don't know what I'm supposed to hear. You say it's music, but then you say you can feel it, like it's a part of the environment."

"It is," Melinda insisted, "it's everywhere, describing the place where you are. Why else do you think music is identified with places like Ireland and Spain and Mexico and China and Africa? It's because that's the way the place sounds."

"There is a strange kind of sense to it all. I do associate certain sounds with places, but in all my travels I can't say I've actually heard music in the air."

"You just have to learn how to listen for it," Melinda pleaded.

"It all sounds lovely, but you must admit that it's also a bit fantastic," smiled Harmony.

Melinda crossed her arms angrily. "My mother says that a lot of fantastic stories are actually based on real things. The ones about people being able to change into different creatures, for instance—like Athenites! Why can't you believe that the story you were named after is also about something real?"

"I want to believe that. Maybe only some people can hear it. Like the Ch'ing-wa Sheng ability that Augusto said you have…you can see Athenites by looking into their eyes, no matter what form they take. I can't do that and will never be able to. It's your gift. Maybe hearing *He Aeros Musike* is a special gift, too."

"*He Aeros Musike*! I haven't heard that in years," a voice said in amazement, startling both of them as Joe walked into the conservatory. "I was on my way to the library when I saw the lights were still on down here. What are you two up to?"

"We happen to be talking about the reality behind the story," Harmony sighed.

Joe squinted. "*He Aeros Musike*? My mother, Harmony's grandmother, used to tell us the story about music in the air all the time."

"Melinda insists she can really hear it. She's described it perfectly beyond the story," explained Harmony. "It's really quite fantastic."

"What's fantastic?" Felix asked, coming in behind Joe. "Wow, this place looks great!" He plucked at the green leaves of a hibiscus that days earlier had looked lifeless and brittle.

"*He Aeros Musike*!" Melinda proudly answered.

Felix looked from Melinda to Joe. "That's ancient Greek, isn't it?"

"As a matter of fact, it is," Joe nodded, eyeing him suspiciously. "Is that important?"

Felix shrugged. "It's one of the languages I've used to try to translate the journals. If I'm doing it right, it translates into something about air and music. I'm not sure because it doesn't make any sense. The same symbols are in the other journals, but their grouping won't translate the same way."

"It was represented in one of the journals?" Joe asked eagerly "Do you remember which one?"

"Yes, I've kept a notebook. What difference does it make? It doesn't really mean anything, does it?"

"I don't know. It might just be a weird coincidence, but it's worth a look." Joe motioned for everyone to follow him. "I think it's time we all had another look at those journals."

Back in the library, Mulligan was performing a symphony of snorts and whistling snores in front of the dwindling fire. Melinda tiptoed passed him, staring at the rotund professor wheezing and sputtering with each open-mouth snore, his drooping gray mustache twitching as his flabby jowls expanded with each breath. "He looks even more like a walrus," she whispered to Harmony.

Harmony smiled as she observed her colleague. "Shh," she insisted through subdued giggles. "You mustn't say that…he's a—"

Melinda rolled her eyes. "I know, I know…he's a brilliant man."

They joined Joe and Felix at the desk, which was covered in books and manuals on forgotten languages, alongside the four leather-bound Turkish journals.

Felix picked up the thick notebook he had used to

chronicle his work on the translations. The pages were swollen with intricate notations and drawings. "I still don't know why you find this reference to music and air so interesting—it doesn't make any sense to me," he groaned as he thumbed through the pages.

"*He Aeros Musike* is an old fable. It tells of music that Athenites could hear on the wind, and which helped them navigate to distant places," Joe explained. "It's also known as *Ictus Aerius* in Latin."

Felix shrugged. "I've catalogued the contents of each journal into this notebook. The hardest part was to locate a particular page, until I found that in every book, each page ends with a different symbol. Take a look—wave, bird, water…"

He flipped through the pages of two of the journals to demonstrate.

"You can also tell which book you're looking through because on every page, the character on the cover is written as an isolated symbol, not connected to anything else. See, this snake is all by itself, it's on every page of this book, and it's also the picture on the cover."

He held up each journal in turn. The covers were engraved in an intricate vine pattern, and they all looked identical until Felix pointed out identifying keys to each. On the top of one cover was a small bird, almost hidden in the leaves of the vines. Another cover had a flower barely detectable on the far left, about midway up. The third journal pictured a snake on the far right-hand side, wrapped tightly around a stem. The last was perhaps the most difficult to see: near the centre of the bottom of the page was a tiny ant that appeared to be climbing up a vine.

"It might mean something important, but for now I'm using all these symbols to mark my place," Felix explained, almost apologetically. At last he located the references to the music in his notebook. "Here it is. The symbols that I translated into Greek are in the snake journal, page wave."

Joe read through the notations in Felix's notebook, then the corresponding hieroglyphs in the snake journal. He clapped Felix on the shoulder. "Fabulous work!"

"Hang on." Felix oozed with excitement as he thumbed through his notes again. "Here we are…I translated this group into Latin, and if I'm remembering properly, the symbols in this journal," he picked up the one with the bird on the cover, "translate into…into…" He paused as he ran his finger along the grouping of hieroglyphs. "Just as I thought… *Ictus Aerius!*" His moment of jubilation subsided as quickly as it was born, and he slumped down onto the desk chair. "I can't believe it! All this for storybooks," he groaned.

Joe looked at the symbols and examined Felix's translation. "I don't think we're looking at storybooks. In fact, if Melinda's ability to locate music in the air and use that to navigate is defined by these journals, then I think the information on these pages may contain facts that are more extraordinary, both historically and scientifically, than we originally fathomed." Joe patted Felix's shoulder enthusiastically. "Felix, I believed you cracked the code. All we have to do now is figure out what these books are trying to tell us."

Professor Mulligan grunted, snorted, yawned and stretched. "I say…what's happening here? Have I missed anything?"

CHAPTER TEN

The stately grandfather clock clicked once, signaling that the time was about to be announced. Felix looked up in anticipation of the melodious chimes that followed. "Six o'clock…I've been at this all night." He leaned back in his chair, massaging his neck as he rolled his head in a slow circular motion to ease the stiffness that had settled into his muscles. He then turned his attention back to the notes he had just recorded into his notebook. A smile twitched at the corners of his mouth. "There's no mistake," he announced proudly. "I did it!"

"Did what?" Melinda yawned as she shuffled into the library.

"I've unraveled a pattern for the translations." Felix motioned for her to join him at the desk.

Melinda rubbed her eyes as she stumbled over. "Please tell me that you haven't been here all night."

"I couldn't sleep after I found out that some of my translations were correct. Come and see what else I've discovered," he said, not even a hint of drowsiness in his voice. "These are the four languages used to translate the hieroglyphs," he said as he pointed to his notebook. "As you can see, it's a bit complicated. Each book uses a combination of ancient languages—so instead of just writing in

Egyptian hieroglyphs, or Latin, Greek, or Celtic, they used a combination of all of them in every sentence. That's probably why Mulligan had trouble deciphering them."

"What do you mean?" Melinda asked through another yawn.

"When translating an ancient text, you usually find the one language used in the original writing. But the author of these journals used four languages and then developed a pattern for their use. So a single sentence uses a combination of symbols and words from all four languages. It's like reading a book written in English, Greek, Russian and Chinese all at once." He looked up to make sure she was following before he continued. "Someone went to a lot of trouble to prevent anyone from deciphering these journals, although I don't know why they bothered."

He picked up one of the ancient leather bound journals, pointing to the small bird hidden in the vines on the cover.

"This one seems to be about agriculture—they ate some strange stuff back then, like grasshoppers." He laid the book back on the desk and picked up another. "The journal with the snake on the cover tells about the culture of the region—including some really weird things. They seemed to believe that beans contained the souls of people." Replacing the journal on top of the desk, he then pointed to the one with the flower on the cover. "That one has a lot of medical remedies, like tasting urine, snot, or earwax to diagnose a patient."

"Gross," Melinda squealed, taking a step backward.

Felix caught her by the arm. "Wait! You haven't heard about the journal with the ant on the cover. It's a good one…sacrifices," he announced, adding a spooky tremor to his voice.

Melinda pulled away. "I don't want to hear any more!"

"You may like this. They believed that when a human died, their spirit would enter an animal's body. That might be a reference to Athenites!"

"We're not spirits—we're real people!" Melinda snarled, shaking her head angrily.

"I know that, but humans often can't understand reality. And if they can't understand something, they often mask it. They've invented loads of stories to help them accept things that they couldn't explain—like us."

Melinda nodded sadly. "If they found out about us today, they'd think we were from another planet." She pouted as she eyed the papers strewn across Felix's workspace. Several pages of notes were stacked in the far corner. "What are those?"

"They're just random symbols from the journals that don't seem to be connected to anything."

Melinda met his eyes. "They must mean something. Why else would they be there?"

"Of course they were written for some reason," he snapped, "I just haven't figured it out yet." He paused, pushing his glasses back in place. "I could only find one thing in the lot of them that translates, but it doesn't mean anything. Look here." He pointed to a sequence of symbols on one page. "In the bird book, it reads KASHDUNE in Greek." He flipped through his notes. "In this journal it translates into KASHDUNE in Latin. In the snake journal it's KASHDUNE in Celtic, and here," he pointed to his notes titled *Flower Book*, "it translated again into KASHDUNE, only this time in Egyptian."

"What does it mean?"

"I don't know. I've looked it up in all the reference books I can get my hands on, but I can't find anything. It's kind of weird. The other weird thing is that the word is always connected to those random symbols that I can't translate into words no matter what I've tried. I even tried using English."

Melinda ran her finger along a line of his notations, reading out the individual letters. "E…e…g…f…c… c…c…" A smile curled the corners of her mouth as she looked back at her brother. "It does remind me of…" Her voice trailed off as she dragged her finger along line after line of the letters, absentmindedly humming an eerily familiar melody. With a self-satisfied grin on her face, she turned back to Felix. "Did you hear that?"

Felix turned toward the doorway, and then looked over at the clock. It was seven thirty. "You probably just heard someone getting up."

Melinda stared unblinkingly at her brother. "Didn't you hear what I was humming?" she asked.

Felix rolled his eyes. "I tried not to."

"What I was about to say a minute ago was that the letters reminded me of musical notes, so I was humming the sounds that the letters would make if they were." She looked at the blank expression on her brother's face. "The melody that corresponds to those notes is the music in the air that identifies where we are!"

Felix nervously fidgeted with his spectacles. "*He Aeros Musike*?"

"Yes!" Melinda pointed to a line of letters, humming as she ran her finger along the page. "It's the music of Paris."

"This is too freaky," Felix sighed. "First, because I didn't think that I believed that stuff about music in the air, and second, because why would the music that supposedly identifies Paris be recorded in hieroglyphs found in journals written thousands of years ago in Turkey?"

"I don't know, but you said yourself that you found references to *music in the air* in every journal. And if you read the letters as musical notes"—she pointed to the page she had just read—"they sound just like the music I can hear…the music that identifies this place."

Felix tapped his pencil on the desk as he pondered this bizarre concept. "That might mean that the rest of the letters identify music of other places," he mumbled, then sat bolt upright. "And if the story of *He Aeros Musike* is true, then these melodies might actually be musical maps!" He jumped to his feet and grabbed Melinda by the shoulders. "That might be the connection!"

"The connection to what?"

Felix sat back down and fumbled through his notes, then pointed triumphantly to a group of symbols. "Kashdune! In every journal the word *Kashdune* is followed by these random symbols, which you are suggesting are musical notes." He paused as he thought over his idea. "Which might mean that if you follow that musical map, you will find Kashdune. And if that's the case, then the rest of this information about how people lived was all just a smokescreen—a kind of camouflage to hide what the books were really all about. Which leads me to think that Kashdune was something very important." Felix looked seriously at his sister. "If you really can hear navigational music, do you think you could follow this kind of trail?"

Melinda shrugged. "I suppose so, but which one? Looking at all these letters that you've recorded from each journal, I can tell that all the melodies are different." She lifted a sheet of paper titled *Random Letters/Flower* and began humming the note connected with each letter. When she finished, she sang through the notations for the other journals.

Felix leaned on his elbows, listening painfully to his sister's quirky concert. When she had hummed the last note of the last journal, he raised his head slowly, a fiercely determined expression on his face. "They're all the same… at their end." He gathered the four journals, placing them in the shape of a cross. "Remember when I said I used the pictures on the covers to determine what journal I was referring to?" he asked excitedly. "The bird is at the top of the cover, the ant at the bottom, snake on the right and flower on the left!"

Melinda grimaced, "You showed me that last night."

Felix smiled. "There may be a musical map inside

these journals leading to something called Kashdune." He tapped each journal. "Look at the pictures now. If all these characters were pictured on a single page, look what you'd have: bird north, ant south, snake east, and flower west! It's a compass!" His glasses had slipped down to the tip of his nose, but he didn't bother to push them back into place. "The first melody you hummed was the music from the bird book…north. But we still don't know which way to travel; do we continue north, or go south? Is there anything in the rest of the music from that journal that identifies another place you've…ah…heard before?"

Melinda picked up Felix's notations and sang through the entire song from the bird book. "This line sounds like something I've heard before," she said, pointing to letters about three-quarters of the way through the piece.

"Do you remember where it was?"

Melinda cringed. "Not exactly, but I think we might have been on holiday. I remember it being hot. I played in white sand and there was gentle surf…it must have been the sea. The water was warm."

Felix bit his lip as he pondered her description. "It's a starting point, anyway. Mom and Dad may have an idea of somewhere we've been that fits that description. My guess would be south of here. It does seem to clarify one thing: the key to using these maps is to identify where you are relative to the location of Kashdune. In our case, it seems that we are north, so we would use the melodies in the bird journal and follow the music that leads southward."

Melinda's eyes sparked. "If it is a map, and the music leads to this thing called Kashdune, *and* if the story of Athenites using music to navigate is true, then maybe this Kashdune has something to do with our ancestry!"

"Precisely." Felix smiled with an uncharacteristic twinkle in his eyes. "Precisely."

The clock struck eight just as Joe walked into the room. "Good morning, you two. I had the strangest thought this morning that those journals are about to tell us something extraordinary."

Out of the corner of her eye, Melinda glanced at Felix, and then turned to greet Joe with an all-knowing smile. "You're absolutely right, Joe. Now come and sit down and we'll tell you exactly what it is."

CHAPTER ELEVEN

"We can't all just transform and fly off following this music of yours," Jake insisted on Monday while Melinda paced in front of him. On Tuesday, speaking from behind his newspaper, he offered, "We need to study this musical phenomenon before we go chasing melodies." By Thursday he called over his shoulder as he left the house, "We don't have the money right now, but we'll continue our research, and when our finances are in order…" He had so many bitter excuses in response to Melinda's incessant pleas for an immediate expedition to Kashdune.

"It's so unfair," she complained to Felix, who only grunted his unsatisfactory reply.

"We'll have to be patient," he said through clenched teeth.

Melinda wasn't in the mood to be patient, and she had the feeling that her brother really wasn't either, mainly because he hadn't argued with her when she snarled, "Patient for *what*? Maybe I should go it alone…I'll be the one to find Kashdune." But she didn't take off on her adventure, instead finding refuge in the conservatory where she sulked away the hours.

One morning, well before the clock struck nine, Melinda, as usual, trooped down to the conservatory. As she rounded the last corner in the hallway, she was hit with the most powerful déjà vu of her life as a gaggle of brittle leaves tumbled toward her. Dumbstruck by what seemed like the same parade of foliage she had experienced only weeks before, and somewhat spellbound by the sight of a bright pink flower, caught in an invisible whirlwind, spinning at her feet, she was frozen in place.

Frightened—not by the leafy procession but by the cause of such a spectacle—Melinda crept slowly forward. Shaking from head to toe, she looked beyond the pirouetting petals and noticed that the door, which she was convinced she had shut the night before, stood open. "What's going on," she whimpered as the circus of foliage danced in the hallway. But when the next parade of petals flew out into the passageway, she had a totally different reaction. "Those aren't dead leaves," she gasped as the green foliage skipped haltingly along. "Somebody has been messing with my plants!"

A myriad of predators paraded through her mind, each one vying to become her creature of choice. Her movements froze for only an instant as fur and claws and sparkling white fangs invaded her body. Her transformation complete, she stepped confidently into the windswept conservatory.

At first glance, nothing had changed since the day before. The door and windows were shut and nothing appeared out of place. Still the breeze swirled through the room. The sound of rustling leaves to her left gave her a clue. Muttering to herself in a low growl, she pulled her lips back to bare her frighteningly T-Rexian teeth. Then she stalked over to investigate.

Three clay pots lay broken on the tiled floor. A pink azalea, its roots shaken free of soil, lay next to a trail of ivy thrown clear of its urn, along with the sad remains of a geranium that had been crunched under someone's heavy foot. Particles of dirt were being blown into the air by the great breeze from the window, which was perhaps the most curious thing of all: the entire floor-to-ceiling glass pane was gone. There were no glass fragments or shards to suggest that it had been broken—nothing, in fact, to suggest that it had ever been there.

She spun around, forgetting for a moment that her body included a rather large, bulky tail. More pots crashed to the floor as she clumsily maneuvered through the rows of plants. Even as this one-girl wrecking crew demolished an entire row of coveted horticultural prizes, she didn't slow her pace.

Out in the hallway, her impressive claws clicking against the marble floor, she loped along the passageway and skidded around the corner. A sound that could only be likened to a low, rumbling bray exited her mouth as she called to Felix, whom she felt certain, must be in the library. She was right.

Ever so tentatively, Felix poked his head out into the hall, pulling it back immediately when he saw the creature rampaging his way. Without considering his movements he seemed to fly across the room, leaping up the stairs. By the time Melinda arrived, Felix had climbed to the second-floor gallery, shivering as he crouched beside the banister, squinting to see what was happening below him. The awesome sight brought tears to his eyes as choking laughter caused him to temporarily lose his breath.

"There's been another break-in," Melinda howled.

Felix stood up, leaning over the railing as he wiped the tears away. There she stood, his sister in all her glory, bits of torn clothing still clinging to her body. "What are you doing?" he managed through fits of giggles. "Let's see what we have here…the front half of you must be at least part tiger—frankly the stripes gave you away. I must say, however, that your mouth doesn't go with the fur…maybe a bit lizard, which does fit with your crocodilian bum!"

"THERE HAS BEEN ANOTHER BURGALARY!" she growled incessantly.

Felix squinted as he listened to the series of grunts, growls, and hoots that came from his sister as she paced the room. He shrugged as he made a slow decent down the staircase; there was nothing in her sounds or movements that he could understand at all. The way things were going, he didn't think that was about to change because every time he yelled to her, "I can't understand you," she would simultaneously yell back in some unfathomable tongue.

He reached the bottom of the stairs as Melinda reached the desk, and she spun around quickly to face him. Once again she forgot about her tail. As her body came about, her tail swung across the top of the desk, sweeping everything off—books, papers, pens, and pencils flew in all directions.

"Melinda you stupid…THING!"

This she understood, and immediately froze to return to human form. Tattered bits of what had been her clothing drifted to the floor, leaving Melinda shivering in the centre of the room. Seconds passed before she realized that she was standing there completely naked. "Felix! Give me your shirt!"

With a snarl and a groan he pulled his favorite black t-shirt—the one with Albert Einstein winking on the front—over his head and threw it to her. "As soon as you put it on, get over here and help me with this mess! I organized everything last night, and now *you* are going to do it!"

Sheepishly, Melinda did as she was told, collecting all the loose papers that had floated a surprisingly great distance away. It hadn't taken long to pick up every last paperclip, but to Melinda's surprise Felix was still scuttling around on the floor. "What are you looking for now?"

Felix stood up, his expression a mixture of anguish, anger, and fear. "The journals aren't here," he gasped with a quiver in his voice. "They were here last night, and I'm sure no one has looked at them this morning."

"Surely someone has them," she suggested as she bent down to survey the floor again.

Felix shook his head, his normal pale complexion turning chalky. "I saw everyone at breakfast. Dad said that he didn't want to hear another word about Kashdune or the journals until they were ready to move forward with something. It was obvious that no one in this household was even entertaining the thought of looking at those books."

"Well then," Melinda announced huffily, "they got their wish, because now the journals are gone." Her smug expression changed instantly as her memory clicked on. "Oh no," she gasped, "I almost forgot what I had come to tell you…someone has broken into the house again!"

After she explained the scene in the conservatory, Felix slumped into the desk chair, rubbing his forehead with one hand and tapping a pencil on the desk with the other. "You think someone has stolen the journals?"

Melinda shrugged. "I don't know, but someone did come into the house last night, and the journals are gone this morning."

Felix nodded. "Which means that we were right—those journals contain information that is somehow valuable."

"Kashdune!" Melinda clapped her hand over her mouth.

Felix nodded. "I think that's highly likely. Luckily we still have our notes…it doesn't look like they took any of those." Just to make sure, he began shuffling through the notes. Satisfied that everything was accounted for, he looked over at his sister. "From what you described, it looks like this thief is no ordinary burglar."

"They're probably professionals. This is getting scary."

"The real scary part is that someone knew about the journals, as well as the fact that we had them—which means that someone has been watching us."

The alley was dark and smelled of rubbish. From the stench, it was also likely that more than one kind of animal had used it as a urinal. The light from the streetlamp didn't extend into this narrow space between two ancient buildings, making it difficult to discern the features of the person standing just inside the opening.

On the street outside, Augusto Chambers hurried along the sidewalk. He was dressed in a dark overcoat with its collar turned up and wore a hat pulled down low across his brow. In one hand he carried a small satchel, in the other a shoebox tied with loops of string. When he reached the alley, he stopped and cleared his throat, then asked in a deep, raspy voice, "Are you there?"

The figure inside the alley stepped out with a nod.

"Mission accomplished," Augusto said, holding up the satchel and box.

"You got them all?" the man from the alley asked.

"Four of them. That's right, isn't it? There were only four?"

The other figure nodded. "And our little friend?"

Augusto held up the shoebox. "I took care of him."

"What do you mean?" the man from the alley demanded, his voice rising. "I told you I need him alive."

Augusto snorted. "He is alive—just incapacitated for a while. I used a little ether, just enough to make transporting him more comfortable."

The man in the shadows sighed, his shoulders relaxing. Then he nodded and drew an envelope out of his coat pocket. "My end of the bargain. My friends will meet you in Nice, at the train station. Here's your ticket, and a little money to get you started." He gave Augusto the envelope, and in turn Augusto handed him the satchel and the box.

"We both got what we wanted, and no harm has been done," the figure said softly.

"We did indeed," Augusto agreed as he opened the envelope under the streetlamp to examine its contents.

"I want to thank you," the man from the alley said, stepping forward and extending a hand. "Your actions will have effects far greater than you can know."

"May I not live to regret that," Augusto replied, looking pleased with himself.

They shook hands and walked in opposite directions down the street.

CHAPTER TWELVE

Darkness had fallen hours ago. From the loud voices and laughter outside the window, the area's nightlife seemed to be just beginning. In this part of the city, singing and loud music rang in the streets into the wee hours. The neighborhood was lively in spite of its shabbiness.

The room itself was dark, dank, and dreary—hardly the type of accommodation Horace Stumpworthy had regularly experienced. In his dirty little cage, he shook and shivered, dreaming of his days of freedom and power. His incarceration in his own laboratory had seemed simply a challenge. Now visions of escape were fading into hopelessness. Even if he could escape his cell, where could he go? He didn't even know where he was. To escape this room, this building, would mean increased danger from animals and humans. His ability to negotiate the streets of Paris, if he was still *in* Paris, as a lemming was greatly hampered. Still something pushed forward, mainly his appetite for hatred. Joe Whiltshire had done this to him— Joe and those stupid Huttons.

"Hello, Horace." The voice was familiar, but Stumpworthy couldn't place it immediately. "Sorry about the accommodation. There have been a lot of changes since we last saw each other...*you*, for example!"

A laugh followed, sending a shock of recognition through Stumpworthy's white, furry body. His eyes fixed on the features of an almost forgotten face as Fredrick Hamsong leaned closer. Hamsong's caramel complexion and thin, clean-shaven face hadn't aged a day since he had seen him last, nearly twenty years ago.

"So it's wolfbane that's done this to you." Hamsong chuckled warmly. "I don't know if I can reverse the infection, but I'll try. After that, we can get to work. And we have a lot of that to do, my friend. A lot to do."

The curtains of the small flat were drawn. Horace Stumpworthy cracked his eyes open, closing them again quickly—even the dim light was blinding. He felt better today; the fever had abated and his muscle pains were beginning to relax.

His mind muddled through his circumstance. He had no knowledge about what had transpired in the world; let alone what had happened to him. He didn't even know what day it was. He could only remember Fredrick Hamsong making him drink something. Whatever it was, it had changed everything. He thought it was simply water, but the convulsive reactions in his body proved otherwise. He was human again. He held up his hand and wiggled his fingers. He would have smiled at the sensation, but even this small movement tired him. He drifted back to sleep for an instant.

"Horace. I thought you'd be awake by now," Fredrick Hamsong said, standing over his prone form. "We've got to get you going again. I need your special talents to save something I believe may be in imminent danger of destruction." Stumpworthy stared up at him weakly. Hamsong shrugged. "I'm not certain how to prepare you for your new life. It will be difficult for you. The process that restored you to your human form also destroyed your ability to transform into anything else."

A car horn sounded outside, pulling Fredrick Hamsong's gaze away in time to miss the confused look on Stumpworthy's face change to anguish, and then, very quickly, to rage.

Felix climbed the stairs, his arms laden with books, his footsteps heavy and his mind deep in thought. What a difference a day made—or in this case, a few hours. When his parents had learned about the break-in and its likely connection to the missing journals, they flipped their thinking over to his and Melinda's. Time was of the essence to discover more about Kashdune before whoever was in possession of the journals beat them to it. Joe had been convinced that Augusto Chambers was their thief, so it was conceivable that anything having to do with Athenite history might be destroyed, just as Augusto and Horace Stumpworthy had done in the past.

Of course there was still the problem of financing an expedition; it was not going to come cheaply, and money was something that the group, even collectively, didn't have. Felix, however, remembered what his father had always said: "Where there is a desire to accomplish something, there is a means to do so." As those words rang in his memory a sly smirk lit Felix's stoic face. "When it's your parents' desire, that is," he chuckled to himself.

As their father squabbled with Joe and Harmony about the best approach for the expedition and Melinda was being escorted by their mother around the city to *listen* for bits of the musical map, Felix was left with little to occupy himself. Replacing the books in the library that they had used for the translations was the only thing he could think of doing for the time being. Plodding up and down the staircase, he worked diligently until he had replaced the last volume on the last shelf on the top floor of the library.

With nothing else to demand his attention, Felix ambled along the bookshelves, looking for something to occupy his mind. Dragging his finger through the thick layer of dust that encased the shelves, he snaked a trail across volumes on biology, geology, meteorology, zoology, and astrology until he came across *The Study of Mythical Archeology*, by Professor Horace Stumpworthy.

Felix pulled the book off the shelf. The cover showed a picture of an ancient statue of the Greek goddess Athena. He flipped the book over to look at the back cover. A picture of the author, the debonair Horace Stumpworthy, smiled back at him.

His first impulse was to pitch the book back onto the shelf, but he didn't do that. He couldn't take his eyes off the image of his former hero. He recalled the first time he'd met the professor, an episode that would be forever etched in his mind. Stumpworthy had been a tall, impressive character: suave, sophisticated and brilliantly self-assured. His face, with its chiseled features and intelligent expression, dark, trustworthy eyes, and black hair only just beginning to gray at the temples, was one of the most memorable faces Felix had ever seen. Everything about the man was indelibly recorded in Felix's mind. From their first handshake to the way the professor moved across a room, commanding respect everywhere he went.

The cruise down memory lane was taking its toll; Felix found himself lightheaded and disoriented, and he grabbed onto the bookshelf to steady himself as his vision blurred. Shadows seemed to be falling across his eyes. His head dropped forward; his glasses fell to the floor. A tingling sensation attacked his entire body, and his breathing came in short, staccato gasps. By the time he thought about panicking, the spell had passed, fading away as quickly as it had come.

Bewildered and a teensy bit worried, he decided that, while panicking was no longer warranted, it was probably wise to abandon his recollections. Without looking again at the book in his hand, he slid in back into place on the shelf. Then he noticed, for the first time, that this particular area contained a lot of books written by Professor Horace Stumpworthy—book after book, shelf after shelf, all by this one incredible, albeit evil, man.

Felix shook his head to dislodge any images that might play havoc in his mind. The movement also caused him to reach up and straighten his glasses, as was his habit to do. Only his glasses weren't there, which he thought quite impossible since he couldn't read without them and he had done just that a minute ago. Then, as his stomach began to flutter and his palms began to sweat, he realized something equally as disturbing. As he patted his face in search of his specs, he felt something quite rough…like the rugged stubble of a very mature beard.

Those weren't the only things that appeared a bit different from the way things were when he had gotten up that morning. For when he glimpsed his hands, as they moved away from his face, he noticed that they weren't his hands at all. These aberrations were large, with trace amounts of dark hair on their backs and smooth calluses on their palms. These were adult hands, not his. But they certainly were responding to his commands as he wiggled the fingers.

"Okay, Felix, don't lose control," he wheezed as he stumbled back to the stairs. "There is a simple and logical explanation for this. I'm probably just dreaming…ha! That's it! I'm having some wild *Rip Van Winkle* dream!" He cautiously negotiated the staircase, slapping his cheeks occasionally in an attempt to wake up from this incredibly vivid nightmare.

When he reached the ground floor, nothing had changed—those hands were still connected to his wrists, and the stubble was still clinging to his face. No matter what he did he could not seem to wake himself, which made him wonder if maybe he wasn't dreaming after all.

He shuffled across the floor, playing over the circumstances that had led up to this bizarre ending. He recalled looking at that book, Horace Stumpworthy's book, and he remembered his thoughts. "It can't be," he wheezed as he walked purposefully over to the mirror that hung above the fireplace, diverting his eyes until he could work up his courage for a peek.

When he did, his fears were confirmed. There it was: the incredible image of Professor Horace Stumpworthy, looking wide-eyed and confused, gawking back like a thirteen-year-old boy.

CHAPTER THIRTEEN

The frightened scowl on Stumpworthy's face changed into a bemused smirk as Felix proudly analyzed his accomplishment. In the past he had rejected the notion that he would ever have even the slightest desire to transform into anything. Throughout his early adolescence—which was usually the time when young Athenites found their thoughts wandering and their bodies following—he had taken the greatest care to control his thinking. He had no desire for the surprise of an unwanted tusk or antler to pop out of his head or the undesirable growth of feathers or fur to cover his body, and he certainly had no wish for flippers or hooves to replace his feet. So this unplanned transformation into the perfect likeness of Horace Stumpworthy should have upset him. But it didn't. Instead, he felt rather proud of himself.

It appeared that he had accomplished what he believed no one else could. At least, he had never heard about Athenites mastering the art of transforming their appearance into that of another person. He bubbled with self-admiration, as he was quite sure that no one in his family had the ability to do so, and he was relatively certain that none of their friends could, either.

"I truly am amazing," he gloated to himself as an

evil smile invaded his expression. "Won't everyone be surprised to see their old friend," he chortled wickedly. "I can't allow Melinda to look into my eyes…she'll tell everyone it's me. Mulligan's going to have a heart attack." He laughed until he realized that that was a real possibility. "Dad will be okay, he's always calm, but Mom…she might rip my throat out first and ask questions later."

Deep furrows began creeping across his forehead as he assessed the less humorous side to the reactions he might get from the other members of the household. "Harmony will punch my lights out; she's quick enough to do it before I can explain." He shook his head slowly as he realized that Joe might present an even more dangerous proposition. "He hates Stumpworthy even more than the others," he whispered. "Whatever he does will be extremely unpleasant for me."

He paced in front of the mirror, glancing up from time to time to regard his reflection. "Maybe I shouldn't spring this on them." He shrugged, and then stopped pacing to admire the startling likeness of the professor staring back at him. "That's it!" He snapped his fingers, smiling sinisterly. "I don't have to surprise them by being *him* first…I can be me and *then* him! They'll still freak out," he assured himself at about the same time that the shrill scream erupted from behind him.

On the other side of Paris, Horace Stumpworthy sat alone in the small kitchen. In a few minutes, he would be leaving the place forever. This small and dingy accommodation held only one significant memory: his human life was restored, but he wondered at what cost.

He heard the sound of the front door opening and closing, followed by exactly ten footsteps echoing throughout the tenement as Fredrick Hamsong moved across the tiny sitting room and into the kitchen. He looked very pleased with himself. "We're ready to go. I've reserved the tickets, but we'll need money for the journey. We'll go to your bank and withdraw a suitable amount."

Stumpworthy looked at his old friend and former colleague. They had worked at the university together years earlier; both had been new professors whose friendship was built on mutual respect for their scientific accomplishments. They lost touch when Hamsong left for a new position at another institution. How strange to have him back in his life now, when so much had been ripped away from him.

"I should probably close the account if I'm to leave Paris," Stumpworthy said in a grave tone. "I can convert the money to your currency when we arrive."

"I'm afraid that will be impossible. Where we're going, your money will have no value."

"What do you mean, no value? What am I supposed to do?"

"We have a currency based solely on our own economy, since we don't trade outside our borders—for obvious reasons. But you're a clever man; I'm sure you'll figure out something."

Life kept getting worse, as did Stumpworthy's mood. "Exactly how am I supposed to do that?"

"We have young people, too—you can teach, as you've done here." Hamsong held his hand up in an *after you* gesture.

Stumpworthy gloomily stood up. He hadn't made his fortune by teaching, and he had no desire to do so now. He might own a science school, but he thought it beneath him to actually interact with the students.

"We'd better get to the bank quickly. We need enough for food and provisions, airfare, and boat hire. I'm sure there are more incidentals, so you'd better take out a generous amount."

Fredrick Hamsong held the door open for Stumpworthy, and the two exited the small room for the last time.

As the impressive pink marble columns of the bank loomed ahead, Felix's resolve weakened. Accessing Stumpworthy's bank account by transforming into the professor's image had seemed like an excellent idea an hour ago. But reality always had a way of raining on the parade of seemingly brilliant ideas.

This particular idea had come to Felix soon after his mother had seen the image of Horace Stumpworthy reflected in that mirror. Of course she screamed. Not the kind of scream you hear in the movies, when a woman cries out in fear—this was more like an all-out declaration of war. Horace's expression was pricelessly helpless as he prepared for his doom…a fate that did not materialize, due to the matter-of-fact explanation offered by Melinda, who stood at their mother's elbow. It was one of those rare occasions when Felix was actually happy—and in this case ecstatically relieved—to see his sister staring into his eyes.

Several minutes passed as Felix suffered the intense scrutiny of his mother and sister circling around him, looking him over from head to toe and back again. They confirmed what he already knew: that he was an exact replica of the famous Professor Horace Stumpworthy. This amazing confirmation did more than feed Felix's ego—it also gave him an idea.

"If I look just like him, maybe we can use this to our benefit," he announced with a wink. "He must have millions in the bank, just rotting away. Lemmings don't have a lot of use for money…but we do." He then explained his plan to access those millions by masquerading as Horace

Stumpworthy. "You said yourself that I look just like him, and I know I can master his signature, as well as mimic his voice. We can make all those millions work for us and set off for Kashdune!" It had taken only minutes to convince his mother, and off they went, leaving Melinda behind to tell the others the news.

That was then—but this was, quite inescapably, now. As Felix and his mother ascended the steps up to the imposing institution that housed Stumpworthy's fortune, his proud expression evaporated. He was still the perfect image of the powerful and stoic Horace Stumpworthy, but without the calm demeanor characteristic of the man. With each step he trembled just a little bit more, his strong appearance weakening into something resembling someone who, after greedily biting into a juicy apple, has noticed the half a worm left behind.

Elaine looped her arm through his for support and pulled him forward toward the ornately carved double doors. "Come on…just a few more steps and we'll be at the security check-in. My research shows that this bank uses a system based on visual imaging."

"I'm not so sure this is going to work," Felix whispered, slowing his pace with every step.

"It's worth a try. If you can get through the first checkpoint, you've made it. The rest is just signatures, and you've mastered that. You can sign his name as well as he could." Elaine tugged her son up the few remaining steps. "All you have to do is look straight into the camera when we get inside."

They entered the building, coming face to face with a meek-looking security guard seated at a small desk. He smiled at them and didn't seem too menacing until Felix noticed the bulge underneath his jacket. "He's got a gun!" he whimpered into his mother's ear.

Elaine dug her fingers into his arm. "There's the camera, just look into it," she whispered back. Felix stared into the unblinking eye of the camera, his skin shimmering with perspiration.

The guard cleared his throat and pushed his chair back, sending a spine-tingling screech across the marble floor. He adjusted his jacket as he stood and leaned across the desk. "*Pardon, madame et monsieur...*"

All Felix could hear after that was an explosion of French words that seemed to blend together into one long, hostile-sounding tirade. He continued to stare into the camera, avoiding the eyes of the officer. Now visibly shaking, he prepared himself for the barrel of that gun to be thrust into his back.

"*Merci!*" Elaine smiled at the guard and pulled Felix in through the open door.

"What was that all about?" Felix stammered as soon as they made it through to the bank itself.

"Felix, I'm surprised at you…have you forgotten your French? He simply said that the camera is temporarily not connected to the door. After the computer confirmed your identity, he pushed a button and, *voila,* the door opened." Elaine began to chuckle. "I got the impression that the guard doesn't appreciate the new security system very much. He says it's always breaking down…I haven't heard that many swear words outside of a football game in ages."

Horace Stumpworthy watched the blur of buildings whiz by from his seat in the back of the sleek white limousine. It wouldn't be long before they would arrive at the bank. He closed his eyes, resting his head against the seat back as a cold, tingling shiver prickled over his body. Life had dealt him a horrific blow. He was destined to live life as a despicable human, without the ability to transform—

without position, without riches, without prestige. How was it possible that Fredrick could hold such power over him? How could his perfect life have dissolved into this nightmare?

The sick feeling of loathing continued to build like a disgusting vapor that seeped into every crevice of his mind. It was beginning to make him feel ill, but Horace didn't back away from his miserable obsession. In fact, he did quite the opposite. He conjured up more images to fuel his hate-filled fancy. Joe Whiltshire, the Huttons, Harmony Melpot, and dithering old James Mulligan danced ceremoniously into his head, each wearing a grotesque smile as they paraded around and around. "They have done this to me," he growled as his jaw tightened and his fists clenched. His once-handsome face screwed up into the ugliness of rage.

Then the pain came—a pain so intense that it made breathing more difficult. His fingers went numb and his body shook uncontrollably.

"Fredrick," he whispered desperately, "something is wrong with me. I can't breathe!" Absolute panic had replaced his anger as he struggled for each gasp of air. Painful spasms raced through his body, and his throat tightened, making both swallowing and breathing increasingly painful. His complexion became sallow; sweat beaded on his forehead and upper lip.

Hamsong looked over calmly, sighing as he reached into his pocket. He pulled out a small metal flask and handed it over. "Sorry, old friend. Drink a little of this…you'll be fine in a minute or two."

Stumpworthy eagerly sloshed the liquid into his mouth, dribbling some down his chin.

"Careful…we don't have much of that left, and we have a long way to go before we can replenish the supply." Hamsong put the flask back in his pocket. "You must try to avoid strong emotions for a while; they can have adverse effects while your body is still recovering. Wolfbane has a violent impact on Athenites. It will take some time before you are completely well."

Horace Stumpworthy did feel remarkably better after the first swallow. Only seconds later, as the car pulled to a stop in front of the bank, he was feeling as near to one hundred per cent as could be expected.

"That must be a miracle drug," said Horace with amazement.

Fredrick chuckled. "It is indeed."

"I would be interested to know a bit more about it," Horace said with a sly smile.

"You will very soon, but first things first." Fredrick opened the car door and stepped out onto the pavement. "Shall we?" he said, motioning toward the bank.

Stumpworthy joined him, still reeling from the effects of the magical elixir. As they climbed up the steps toward the magnificent pink marble columns and beautifully carved doors, he looked wonderingly at his companion. *Maybe life still has some elements of interest after all*, he thought as he followed Fredrick through the entrance.

The security door that led into the bank was just closing, giving a glimpse of the backs of a man and woman as they disappeared through. Horace's lip curled as he watched them vanish from sight. *I'm just like that man now—human*, he thought with disgust, then diverted his attention to look into the security camera. Seconds passed but the doors did not open. The guard mumbled something about the imbecile who had designed the security system, saying that although the computer confirmed his identity, the doors would not open automatically.

"If the computer accepts my identity, then why don't you simply open the doors manually?" Horace seethed through clenched teeth.

The guard shrugged, pushed a red button, and the doors swung open. Horace shook his head and marched purposefully through, followed closely by Fredrick Hamsong.

Felix's confidence was building until he heard the sound of the security door opening behind them. At first his knees wobbled and his stomach tightened. He fought hard to regain his composure, telling himself that whoever was behind them didn't present a threat. Then one of them spoke in an annoyed tone—"inept moron," he said, to which his companion grunted lightheartedly. After that the only sound was the clomping of their hard-soled shoes against the green tiled floor. Felix relaxed. There was nothing in the manner of these people that was menacing.

But then it happened: one of the men behind them clearly pronounced the name *Horace*. For Felix, hearing that name was the same as having the barrel of the guard's gun shoved into his ribs. He slowed his pace in stymied dread, but Elaine grabbed his arm, tugging him forward as she whispered a stern warning. "Don't panic…there are other Horaces in the world. Keep walking and don't draw attention to us."

Felix might have calmed himself at this observation, but for one thing. The same man said "Stumpworthy" before dissolving into a tirade of hushed words that Felix couldn't make out.

If a whip had cracked against their bums, it couldn't have made them walk any faster. Without even glancing behind them, Felix and Elaine bolted down the hallway, taking a sharp right-hand turn down another passageway marked *Conference Room A*.

Watching this spectacle, Horace Stumpworthy shook his head slowly. "They must be late for a meeting."

Fredrick nodded, still staring at the sign for Conference Room A. "It must be an important one. But as I was saying, I appreciate your interest in our 'wonder drug', as you call it and I promise to tell you everything when we arrive at our destination. The quicker we conclude our business here, the quicker all that can happen."

Nearly half an hour ticked by as Felix and Elaine remained hidden in the darkened conference room.

"They recognized me—I mean, they recognized him!" Felix leaned against a wall and slid down into a heap on the floor.

"Maybe they were just talking about him. He was a very famous man, and most people don't know he's a rodent... at least, not a furry one." Elaine crossed the room and patted the top of Felix's head. "We shouldn't have panicked. After all, isn't the idea to be recognized as him?"

Felix nodded. "Of course it is," he said, pushing himself back up the wall. "I just wasn't ready to be confronted by someone who really knew him. It's one thing to fool a security camera or a bank clerk, but quite another to deceive a friend. I'm ready now." He strode over to the door, confidently opened it, and motioned for his mother to go through first. "Let's make a withdrawal, shall we?"

His resolve remained steadfast as they walked down the hallway, even when he glimpsed the backs of two men making their way toward the exit. They looked strangely familiar, and he felt certain they were the men who had uttered Horace's name earlier. As they disappeared from view, nothing else rattled him until they entered the transaction lobby and the young man at the counter said, "Mr. Stumpworthy. You're back."

Felix leaned on the counter to steady himself and cleared his throat. Then in his best Stumpworthy voice, he replied, "I haven't been away. But I am taking a holiday now, and I need to withdraw a rather sizeable sum."

The sandy-haired young man winced slightly as a tiny frown creased his forehead. "Yes…of course. It's only…"

He hesitated on the edge of reminding Mr. Stumpworthy that he had just withdrawn a sizeable sum only minutes before.

He recalled the lecture he had received from his supervisor earlier that day after a similar situation with an elderly gentleman: "Many of our customers are a bit eccentric," his supervisor had explained, "and some of their requests may sound a little silly. Just remember that it is our job to accommodate them, not advise them."

The young man looked up at Felix and smiled. "Of course, Mr. Stumpworthy. How much would you like?"

CHAPTER FOURTEEN

Fredrick Hamsong relaxed. The first-class cabin of the 747 was more comfortable than he had remembered. Sipping his champagne, he allowed his body to melt into the seat for the beginning of his last journey home.

A glimpse over at Horace Stumpworthy suggested that he was having difficulty doing the same. "I'm sorry your life has taken such an unfortunate turn, Horace," Fredrick said. "Ironic, isn't it, how your bad fortune has actually benefited me."

Stumpworthy looked at Fredrick but didn't respond.

Hamsong turned and glanced out the window. They were now flying thousands of meters above the sea. "I miss flying. I can still remember the sensation, but it's been years…too many years," he said wistfully.

An involuntary shiver rippled through Horace's body. "I must admit, it's still too new to me…I can't imagine life *without* flight. I've never liked this kind of travel," he said, nodding at the airplane cabin. "It's so confining."

Hamsong sighed, resting his head against the seat. "You get used to it. I remember when these things were first introduced. No one really thought they would fly and look at us now! Air travel is everywhere. People can explore the planet in relative comfort and safety. When I was a lad, only Athenites could do that."

Stumpworthy frowned at his companion. "When you were a lad? If I am not mistaken, planes have been around a lot longer than you have."

Hamsong cleared his throat but remained silent. He looked out the window again, then turned back to face Stumpworthy. "I hope you realize I didn't plan it this way. I'm sorry about the loss of your abilities, but it was the only way I knew to cure the poisoning."

Horace looked straight ahead. "I don't blame you, Fredrick. You didn't administer the wolfbane…that was Joe Whiltshire, with the help of Felix Hutton. If it wasn't for you, I'd still be a lemming." He sighed deeply. "I was lucky you found me."

Hamsong chuckled. "Our good friend Augusto Chambers informed me of your ordeal."

"Augusto? Don't you mean Oscar?" Stumpworthy had an evil grin on his face.

"He told me about that, too…Horace, you should be ashamed of yourself, administering such a vile virus to a friend. I hope you're not disappointed, but *Oscar* is no more. Augusto has recovered! It is an interesting phenomenon. It seems that a cure for the virus is to mix antibodies from an immature Athenite with an infected one. When he was the dog, he bit an Athenite youth. As a result, his transformation abilities were restored."

Horace frowned. "Augusto was actually infected by the virus accidentally. I'm pleased he's returned to his old self. As for the antidote, I was made aware it immediately before I was infected with wolfbane." Stumpworthy became sullen, remembering how Joe Whiltshire was cured of being trapped in the body of a rabbit after he bit Melinda Hutton, and the same thing had happened with her father and brother soon after. "An unfortunate defect of the virus," he said with a sigh.

Hamsong frowned. "Horace, I hope that after your own ordeal you have given up on such heinous experiments."

Stumpworthy smiled noncommittally. "So where is Augusto now? Will he be joining us?"

Fredrick shook his head. "Augusto had other plans. He's a changed man from when I knew him years ago. He was such an angry young man back then. Now all he wants is to start over, to make a new life where no one knows him. I promised to help him if he helped me."

"Helped you with what, dare I ask?"

Fredrick stiffened in his seat. "There were certain items I needed retrieved from your old house—you, for one, but also a few things of a more sensitive nature. I tried to destroy them in Turkey, but the Huttons got in the middle of that, I'm afraid."

Stumpworthy snorted. "The Huttons have a knack for getting in the middle of things."

Fredrick gave him a sharp look. "They meant no harm. They had no way of understanding just how dangerous my journals were—to them, and to others. I'm indebted to Augusto for returning them to me."

Stumpworthy looked out the window at the passing clouds. "Augusto and I did some fantastic work together. He was instrumental in the development of the virus."

"Well, there will be no need for any of that anymore," Fredrick said nervously. "Kashdune is safe from the ugliness of this side of the world. It is an Athenite paradise. Of course, there are some humans, but we all live in understanding of one another."

Stumpworthy turned back to his reading, making it clear that the conversation was over. The remaining seven hours of the flight went by in silence.

The rumbling rhythm of the surf greeted Fredrick Hamsong the next morning. He smiled long before his

eyes opened, feeling the warmth of the morning breeze
circulating in the room. When he opened his eyes, his
happy mood disintegrated into despair and he was greeted
by the same despondency that he had felt the night before.
He was alone in this amazingly luxurious room. Glass
French-styled doors opened onto a large stone terrace that
overlooked a private beach of white sand. It was all very
beautiful, but it wasn't home.

There had been a delay in their boat hire that would
cost them at least another week…time that Fredrick knew
he could not afford. Sighing loudly, he swung his legs
painfully over the side of the bed. "We must leave here
today," he grumbled. "There must not be any more delays!"

He found Horace at the poolside restaurant, sitting
alone. A light breeze carried the scent of a hundred
tropical flowers. Sounds of the distant surf mingled with
the splashing of a magnificent waterfall cascading into the
pool. It was as Horace had described it: a blissful retreat in
a tropical paradise.

"Good morning, Fredrick," Horace greeted, unusually
cheerfully. "This is a wonderful place. I've stayed at the
Tropical Beach Mirage Resort for years. It is the epitome
of luxury on this island." He sipped his coffee happily.

"Horace, we don't have time for this…we need to be
on our way."

"You said it yourself—we don't have any transport.
We'll just have to be patient and enjoy our surroundings."
Stumpworthy crunched into a toasted muffin laden with
butter and gooey red jam.

Hamsong slumped into a chair, holding up his hand
to discourage a waiter from filling his coffee cup. "I don't
think you understand…"

Stumpworthy didn't let him finish. "Look, Fredrick.
My entire life has changed. I've gone along with what
you've asked me to do, and I've promised to help you
protect Kashdune. I will even live the rest of my life

on your island. Please, let me enjoy my last few days of freedom. Now, why don't you relax and have some coffee, or would you prefer tea?"

Hamsong massaged his temples with his fingers. "I'm so sorry, Horace, but we must go as quickly as possible." He reached inside his jacket and withdrew the flask, opened it, then tipped it over. It was empty. "This magic elixir is what saved both of us from our separate fates. My life is dependent on drinking it daily, as is yours. It has granted us both a kind of immortality—without it, we will die. Kashdune has the only supply on Earth. I'm afraid that even one week is far too long to go without."

Stumpworthy's pleasant expression melted into an angry glare.

"I brought enough for my use…I wasn't counting on sharing with anyone." Hamsong replaced the cap and placed the flask back inside his pocket.

Horace slammed down his napkin and stood up. "All right, we'll go. I'll buy a boat and we'll set sail immediately," he said angrily. "I suppose it will be good to have my own yacht to live on, anyway…it'll be better than living in some mud hut on your backwater little island."

The sun had risen to its midafternoon height, and Horace Stumpworthy's beautiful yacht, *The Nautica,* had been underway for at least three hours. Horace was piloting in the direction Fredrick indicated, but as they got farther from land he began to question Hamsong's style of navigation. Fredrick sat facing the bow of the boat. His eyes were closed and he looked like he was asleep.

"Fredrick, if you'd rather nap, why don't you give me the coordinates?"

"I'm not tired…just listening."

"The engines are fine."

"I'm not listening to the engines. I'm listening for the music…the melody that will guide us to Kashdune."

Stumpworthy slowed the speed of the boat. "What *are* you talking about?"

"*He Aeros Musike*—surely your mother told you that story." Hamsong chuckled. "Well, my friend, it's not just a lovely story. It is real, and Athenites have been navigating by those natural harmonies for centuries. It's only in the last few hundred years that they stopped listening. The melodies are always floating on the breezes and will guide you, if you know how to hear them." He closed his eyes again. "I suggest we continue. No matter what happens, continue to follow my directions." He pointed toward the east, and Horace reluctantly accelerated again.

After three more hours of calm water and brilliant sunshine, the weather began to change—quickly. A churning sea rumbled and rolled beneath them. The height of the waves grew alarmingly, violently splashing over the deck as the boat pitched in the unsteady swells. Stumpworthy clicked on the marine radio to pick up a weather report, but the radio was dead. "Maybe we should turn back," he yelled over the noise of the building squall.

Hamsong smiled. "There's nothing to be worried about. I've done this crossing more times than I can count. Just follow the direction I'm giving you." He rose and walked over to stand next to Horace. "Stay the course and don't panic. You'll see…we'll be fine."

As quickly as the sea had become a raging tempest, it mellowed into an ocean of such glassy smoothness that not even the slightest ripple upset its mirror-like quality. Horace slumped into the captain's chair. "I have never seen anything like this. It was like a hurricane only seconds ago…now this! What is going on?" He looked back in the direction from which they'd come and saw only the same glassy water sparkling as far as the eye could see. When he turned back, the glistening water had disappeared again, this time into a milky mist. "What in the world—where did this come from? It wasn't here a minute ago."

Calmly, Fredrick took the wheel and pushed on the accelerator. "I'll take it from here."

"What do you think you're doing? It's like sailing into cotton wool!" Stumpworthy screeched, but no sound was heard. Everything was absorbed by the thick vapors that surrounded them. The deeper they penetrated the white mass, the denser the cloud became, until Horace couldn't see anything, not even the man standing only inches away. He yelled again but there was no sound. Gasping for breath while anxiety and panic swelled in him like a balloon about to explode, Horace felt certain he was about to greet his own mortality. *He's going to kill us* rang in his mind.

Then in a flash of light, the cloud disintegrated. Sun once again reflected off the sea and the sky returned to its timeless blue.

Hamsong was still at the helm, smiling pleasantly. "I told you, old friend—everything will be just fine." He lifted a hand and motioned ahead.

Stumpworthy swallowed the salty air and looked in the direction Fredrick indicated. An island was just visible in the distance. "Kashdune?"

Fredrick nodded. "I don't need the music now." He laughed. "I'm sorry I wasn't able to explain before. I had to concentrate or we would have gone off course, a very dangerous proposition. That was the access we just traveled through—tricky business if you don't listen carefully."

"Good lord! You want to change *that*?" Horace shook his head.

"I think it can be done. If we can change the density of the vapors, we might be able to bend the sound waves. Anyone following the music to Kashdune would be pushed off course. They'd never make it to this side."

Stumpworthy looked back at the cloud, but it was gone. There was nothing but sea and sky. "Where is it? It couldn't just disappear…it was too thick." Stumpworthy was wide-eyed, shivering slightly.

"It's always there. If we followed the precise series of melodies we would see it again."

A long silence ensued as the boat progressed through the smooth water. Horace Stumpworthy was half expecting another bizarre weather front to upset their course, but nothing interrupted their remaining journey. He stared at the island as it slowly came into unclouded focus.

At first it seemed like any other tropical paradise. Creamy beaches and emerald vegetation weren't unique to this island. He'd seen a lot of them in his lifetime. But there was a difference, a quality that he couldn't quite grasp. Miles of sea were behind them now. Kashdune waited ahead. As each minute brought them closer to the shores of this unusual paradise, Horace Stumpworthy felt his pulse quicken and his breathing shorten, a strange sense of excitement overtaking him. *Yes*, he thought. *There is something extraordinary here.*

"Welcome to Tasmay," Fredrick announced, motioning toward the city in the distance. "It is Kashdune's largest city, and has been my home for a very long time."

"It all looks very nice, but I don't understand something. If we are successful in altering the sound patterns, how will anyone be able to navigate through? Surely your citizens will not want to be trapped here."

"We're not trapped here. We're here by choice. The other world has changed in an unpleasant way. There are people who would want to exploit what we have. Our position alone might attract people and governments with hostile intentions. It was decided about three years ago to attempt to close the access. It gave everyone time to sort out their lives—here and on the other side."

Stumpworthy curled his lips. "Forgive me, Fredrick. Maybe you are all here by choice—I, however…"

"Yes, of course…you are not here by a will of your own. Still, I trust you will come to appreciate our world." Fredrick closed his eyes and lifted his face toward the sky, soaking in the warmth of the sun. "It is a shame that we can no longer share our world. I've destroyed all references to the island and its music that existed on the other side— at least those that I know about," he added, looking back toward his island home. "So even if we cannot change the access, Kashdune and its music should remain safely tucked away forever."

"But what if there is someone out there who already knows about the music…what if we change the access and they go off course? What will happen to them?"

Hamsong dragged his eyes away from his beloved Kashdune and frowned at Horace. "That would be unfortunate indeed. Going through the access is like traveling into another dimension. If you went off course, there is no telling what would happen. A person might travel to yet another dimension, or be trapped in some kind of oblivion. I shudder to think of the possibilities. I can only hope that it doesn't happen. We have taken all the precautions we can…and we can do no more."

CHAPTER FIFTEEN

It was hard for Melinda to believe that she had been sitting on an airplane for several hours. Wasn't it only minutes ago that Felix had left for the bank to obtain funds for their expedition? And yet that had been yesterday. It seemed like everything since then had been organized with dizzying speed.

She dropped her head forward and massaged the back of her neck. It was proving increasingly difficult to ignore all the sounds: the roar of the engines, the muted conversations of other passengers, and the loud snorts from Harmony, who was snoring peacefully in the seat in front of her. Perhaps the most difficult noise to ignore was the one in her head: Professor Mulligan's high-pitched shriek of "The Bermuda Triangle—you'd be insane to go there!"

Of course the professor chose not to come along—a sentiment that Melinda not only accepted, she envied. Her resolve to search for Kashdune weakened considerably when she recalled the stories she'd heard about lost ships and airplanes that entered the Triangle. They were never seen again, perhaps gobbled up by a giant sea squid or made into slaves to serve the violent desires of Poseidon, the lord of the sea. "They're just stories," her mother had said to calm her. But that explanation did little to soothe

Melinda's fears, given that her own Athenite ancestry was also classified by many as "just a story."

The islands in the area known as the Bermuda Triangle were the most obvious place to begin their search. Jake and Elaine reckoned it was the place Melinda remembered with warm, sandy beaches—the place where the music matched the melody from the journals. Now, as she jetted through the air, Melinda reluctantly agreed. Even traveling at nearly six hundred miles an hour, she was able to hear the melody, albeit a ridiculously fast-forwarded version.

Melinda sighed when the plane touched down. A quick look out of the window confirmed that they were not inside the stomach of some giant sea monster, and there was no sign of the trident-wielding sea god. It all looked very normal for a tropical island: palm trees swaying in the breeze, exotic flowers in the distance, and bright-colored shirts on the backs of the ground crew that greeted the aircraft.

A taxi whisked them off the airport grounds and drove them toward the hotel where Joe had arranged for them to stay, the Tropical Beach Mirage Resort. "It's my favorite spot on this island—very luxurious, and outrageously expensive. But since Horace has been so kind with his money, it's now quite affordable."

"It's the beginning of the end," Melinda whispered, nestled in the back seat between her mother and Felix.

Felix leaned in closer. "What do you mean?"

"I can hear it…we're at the end of the songs. They're all the same now."

Felix squinted and looked out the window at the blur of tropical vegetation, hotels, and beachgoers. He turned back to face her. "We've found Kashdune?"

She shook her head. "No, it's only the beginning," she whispered sleepily.

"What do you mean…is it the end or the beginning?" Felix demanded.

Elaine looked at her daughter and put an arm around

her shoulders. "Felix, leave her alone for a while…she's exhausted. We'll be at the hotel in a few minutes. After a swim and some relaxation, we can talk about what she's heard." Elaine jerked her chin toward the driver. "In any case, I think it's best if we talk about all of this later."

Melinda slept fitfully, unable to clear her mind as musical impulses chased her through a dark abyss. She awoke in an equally dark room. Her brother lay in the other bed, his face squished into the pillow. She got up and left the room, following the short hallway outside to a large sitting room. On the other side of the suite was her parent's room. Slowly it all came back. After arriving, she'd wanted to rest for just a few minutes, but she had obviously overdone the nap. She knew it would be best to go back to sleep, but the brightening sky outside was too distracting.

She walked back to her room and thought about climbing back in bed, but walked to the door that led outside instead. Sliding the door open as quietly as she could, Melinda stepped out onto a tiled balcony overlooking the beach. The air was just beginning to warm as a thin line of golden light illuminated the horizon. Everything else remained colorless and dark. Melinda was wide awake even at this predawn hour. Part of the reason was the twelve hours of sleep she'd just gotten, but the other reason was the music that swarmed around her. It was familiar and beautiful, an exotic mix and the most luscious melody she had ever experienced. "Kashdune!" she whispered. "It's the beginning of the end of the symphony."

Her nightgown fell to the floor as she instantly transformed and took flight. She didn't think about anything except following the call of the music. It was intoxicating. She seemed to have no choice but to chase that gorgeous melody. She was flying by sound, closing her eyes to feel the sensation of the musical vibration.

Soon she was far out to sea in a tireless flight, and she didn't notice the rising sun as it sparkled on the crystal sea. The light breeze that brushed against the rippling waves didn't attract her attention, nor did the turbulence that followed, sending her bouncing in the invisible currents. Nothing mattered except the call of the siren, the music of Kashdune. Even when the wind increased to a frightening velocity, Melinda flew on, never letting her concentration shift from the music. The howl of the gale-force winds and the violence of the untamed sea didn't deflect her at all. She kept her eyes closed and followed the musical map.

Once more the air settled into calm. And with the calm came a cool, bright dampness where the music was at its most intense. The magical vibration pulled her forward, freeing her mind from the obstacles of fear and doubt. She opened her eyes for the first time in hours and saw the clear sky and mild sea surrounding her. In the distance was an island. The last bit of the symphony was playing on the breeze.

She still felt the pull from the music, but her energy was failing. Time had evaporated and she was tired from hours of flying. She needed to get over land quickly. At last the sandy shore was below her, and the music relaxed into the background of her consciousness.

"Hello?" a boy playing on the beach called up. "Are you new to the island?"

The boy's voice awakened Melinda from her trance, allowing fear to seize control of her thoughts. She didn't know where she was. She didn't know how to contact her parents. She felt vulnerable and very alone. She began to tremble, and then suddenly lost altitude, flapping her wings erratically as she hurtled toward the ground. She crash-landed a short distance from the boy, toppling end over end. The last thing she saw before she sank into

unconsciousness was a figure rushing toward her, sparkling
sand flying from his feet.

Melinda woke, not to sand and surf, but to soft covers
and a warm bed. She stretched her mind before her body
and wondered if anything since leaving Paris had actually
happened. Opening her eyes confirmed that it had. She was
human again, and dressed in silky emerald-green pajamas.
She didn't think she owned any silky emerald-green
pajamas. And this was not her room. She looked around,
quite certain this was not the room at the resort either.

A soft sea breeze made the curtains dance. There
didn't seem to be any glass in the window, and she could
glimpse the beautiful garden that lay just outside the room.
Floral fabrics of greens, pinks, and purples adorned the
furnishings inside the room, which seemed to blend with
the tropical plants that lived both inside and outside.

"You're awake," said a female voice from the doorway
that Melinda assumed led to the rest of the house. Melinda
jerked her head toward the sound, but there was no one
there. "Please don't be frightened. We won't harm you.
We're concerned about you. Where are your parents...
where did you fly from?"

Melinda didn't answer, whipping her head around in
search of the speaker.

"My son Evan found you on the beach. He carried you
to me...I helped you transform and made sure you rested."
The woman was still nowhere to be seen, but her deep,
sensitive voice seemed closer.

Melinda squinted and frowned. She leaned forward,
then to the left, then to the right, spying as far as she
could without leaving the safety of the covers. In a quick,
swooping movement she looked under the bed, but there

wasn't anything, let alone anybody there. Slithering farther under the soft fabric of the duvet, with her bright wide blue eyes as her only recognizable feature, she waited for the woman to show herself.

"I'm sorry, please don't be scared. I'm here next to you…I often dissolve without thinking, and sometimes cause such a stir," the woman laughed. A door opened across the room and a green robe swooped out; Melinda shivered as the garment wrapped itself around the body of an invisible woman.

Seconds later a dark-eyed woman appeared. She was tall, with long, dark curly hair that seemed to shine in the sunlight. Her mouth formed a wide smile, showing off bright white teeth. "My name is Augustina; I'm Evan's mother, and something of a healer around here. Luckily there was nothing wrong with you except exhaustion. It often happens when people come through the access." Melinda sat up stiffly. Augustina continued, "I can see from your expression that you are not used to this type of transformation. I have heard they don't do it on the other side…I've always wondered why. Anyway, I know you're an Athenite, and you must know that we are too. In fact, almost everyone on the island is."

"So I made it," Melinda breathed, hardly daring to believe it.

The woman nodded. "Indeed. Welcome to Kashdune."

CHAPTER SIXTEEN

Clad in his baggy blue-and-black-striped pajamas, Felix shuffled down the hallway and into the large sitting room where his parents were enjoying their morning coffee. "Mawrnin," he yawned.

His mother looked up cheerfully. "Morning. How did you sleep? Do you know it's already ten o'clock? I suppose I'd better get Melinda up...she's been asleep since we got here."

"She's already up," Felix said, stretching and absentmindedly scratching his bum.

Elaine frowned. "She is? That's strange—I've been up for hours and I haven't seen her."

"All I can tell you is that she's not in her bed." Felix stumbled over to a peach-colored sofa and collapsed onto it.

Jake looked up from his coffee, one eyebrow raised. "Felix, did you see her at all this morning?"

Felix shook his head. "Maybe she went to the pool. She probably left a note; she always does."

Elaine nodded. "You're right. But she's been gone a long time. I wish she would have asked me before she went out...I really don't like her wandering around by herself."

"Mom, she's an Athenite. What could happen? Unless of course she transformed into something weird...you know, part dolphin, part pony, with a little mouse mixed in."

Jake snickered in mid-sip, sending coffee up his nose. Elaine scowled at him. "Serves you right!" She looked around the room for a note and then went into her bedroom. She returned in seconds. "She didn't leave a note here, maybe in your room?"

She left Jake sorting out the burning in his nose and Felix becoming one with the sofa. She returned before the scene had changed.

"I couldn't find a note," she announced. "I think we need to go see what she's up to." She sighed as visions of Melinda transformed into a pony-dolphin-mouse *thing* danced in her mind.

Felix moaned as he hoisted himself off the sofa. The last thing he wanted to do right now was hunt for Melinda. As he shuffled back toward his room, he felt unexpectedly anxious, which was strange since he wasn't the least bit concerned about his sister. He glanced back. His mother had left the room and his father was still on the sofa, leaning forward, his elbows balanced on his knees as he massaged his forehead. Felix shook his head. "I don't get it. I feel really weird—like I'm worried about Melinda even though I'm not."

Jake looked up. "You must be worrying by osmosis. Welcome to parenting. Never mind—get dressed, and let's go see where your sister has got to."

Felix dressed quickly in beige shorts that were slightly too small, one of his many message-adorned black t-shirts, black socks, and a sad pair of open-toed sandals. His shockingly white legs gleamed in the sunlight shining in through the open doors to the balcony. As he shoved his pajamas into his suitcase, Felix listened to the rippling sounds of the surf and the shrill cry of gulls from outside. He closed his eyes and listened to all the sounds of the island, hoping to hear something else: the music of Kashdune. There was no music in the air for him.

He looked over at Melinda's empty bed. At the foot of

the bed was her open suitcase, still neatly packed. "What did she mean yesterday—the beginning, the ending?" he mumbled as he looked around as if he expected to see his sister asleep in a corner. He turned to rejoin his parents, but hesitated, glancing back at Melinda's suitcase. "Nothing has been disturbed; she never folds her own clothes, which would mean she hasn't gotten dressed yet," he whispered as his stomach began to churn. He stared at Melinda's belongings until the squawking of several birds outside on the balcony caught his attention.

The birds flew away the moment he approached the doorway, but there was something more interesting than the likes of them heaped in the centre of the deck. Felix recognized it as Melinda's nightgown, and crossed over to it, gingerly tapping the garment with his foot in case Melinda was still inside the fabric. Then, lifting gently with two fingers as if it had cockroaches scurrying all over it, he gasped. Familiar kestrel feathers fluttered out of the folds. "Please tell me that she didn't follow the music," he gasped in disbelief.

"What's keeping you?" Elaine asked, coming up behind him.

He jerked around. His ghostly expression accompanied by the floating feathers answered her question.

"She went in search of Kashdune," Joe said, seated in the Huttons' suite. "The music she hears is very powerful. Somehow I can feel its pull even though I can't hear it."

"How can you be so certain?" Elaine crossed the room to the balcony and looked out at the endless seascape.

Joe shook his head and shrugged. "I can't answer that. It's just a feeling, a very strong feeling. I believe she may have found Kashdune, and I'm convinced she's safe."

Jake was pacing the length of the sitting room, his bare

feet slapping softly on the red tiled floor. "I hope you're right. Let's just hope she's on her way back."

Joe collapsed onto a sofa. "I don't think she is," he said, looking down at the floor.

"Joe! You're not helping," Harmony scolded.

"I'm sorry—but I don't think she is on her way back, and I know she's okay. It sounds ludicrous even to me, but I truly believe what I'm saying." Frowning, Joe stood up and began pacing in the opposite direction as Jake.

"How can you know these things?" Elaine spun around and glared at him.

Joe stopped moving. "Like I said, I don't know, but I know I've had these feelings before. In Turkey, I knew she had arrived in the country; that's why I wasn't at all surprised to see Felix on that mountainside. In the cave, during the explosions, I couldn't see or smell anything—I had to rely on a strange sense that led me to her. Chalk it up to my being her pet rabbit for so long…it's the only explanation I have."

"An intuitive sense," Jake stated flatly.

"Perhaps, but it feels a lot stronger than intuition." Joe hesitated. "It's more of a mind connection."

"Wait a minute," Felix gasped. "The antibodies…that's how you know! You and Melinda might be connected mentally because of the mix of antibodies." Felix joined the parade of pacing, staying even with his father as they marched opposite Joe. "It makes sense." Felix stopped for a couple of seconds and then began his rhythmic parade again, now falling in step with Joe. "When Joe, as Aesop, bit Melinda, we know two things happened: Joe recovered from the virus and Melinda began to mature into her Athenite abilities."

"That's right. The antibodies mixed together and…" Harmony began, but Felix finished her thought:

"—And they both changed. Joe has already said that he knows certain things that Melinda is experiencing, and I happen to believe that she knows things about him as well. When the earthquake erupted in Turkey, Melinda was feeling strange all day. She said she couldn't stop thinking about you and Joe."

"That's right," Jake added, looking perplexed and excited. "It was the day she learned to fly, and she was in a weird funk all day."

"And when we were on that crazy moped in Turkey, Melinda knew how to find the cave you guys were trapped in. I thought she was nuts, but she was right."

Elaine stepped into the middle of the pacing crowd. "It's a nice theory, but it doesn't help us now."

"It might," Felix bubbled.

Harmony leaned forward. "Felix, the same mixing of antibodies happened to you and your father. Is there some connection that you both feel beyond the regular father-son thing?"

Jake and Felix looked at each other, and it was like lightning struck both of them instantly. "This morning," Felix pointed at his father, "when you were on the sofa, I said I felt worried, but I wasn't worried..."

Jake pointed back at Felix. "I was worried! You must have felt my mood!"

Elaine put her hand to her forehead. "It's all very interesting and wonderful that you can all read each other's, minds but what does any of this have to do finding Melinda?"

"Mom, don't you see? If Joe has this strange sense about Melinda, he may know how to find her."

Joe looked helplessly at Felix as everyone looked at him. "I feel positive that Melinda followed the music...I even think she has found Kashdune."

"That would be wonderful," said Harmony.

Joe shook his head. "I may have this connection that Felix is talking about, but I don't know how to find her. She followed the music, and the fact remains that none of us can do the same—none of us can even hear it."

CHAPTER SEVENTEEN

Dressed in a pair of Evan's jeans that were two inches too short and a fuchsia pink blouse of Augustina's that was considerably too big, Melinda ventured outside her room and into the garden. It was an incredible place. As the music of Kashdune surrounded her, mingling with the strange and wonderful song of a multitude of colorful birds, she lost herself in the midst of vibrant flowers that grew against a backdrop of emerald lushness. Even her sense of smell was rewarded with the intensely exotic fragrance of the blooms.

Augustina drifted into the garden as well. "Our garden is one of our many blessings. It's healing to the senses, don't you agree?"

Melinda nodded shyly.

"I can see that you are well and rested. But your spirit suffers." Augustina motioned for Melinda to join her on a green stone terrace. "You are worried."

Melinda nodded again, not looking up as she walked over to a large glass table that stood in the centre of the terrace, surrounded by ornately carved stone pots filled with exotic plants.

"I believe your family must know you are safe," Augustina offered as she sat across the table from Melinda.

"I just want to go back or for them to come here, but they can't hear the music to follow it." Melinda looked up, her eyes glistening with tears. "And I don't think I can follow it back. It sounds so different from here."

Augustina fingered a tangerine-colored orchid resting in the centre of the table. "I'm sorry, but I don't know how to navigate to the other side. I've never been there. Some people go that way, but most of us are happy to stay here."

"Is there a way I can phone them? I need to let them know where I am." Melinda looked up as a single tear trickled down her cheek.

Augustina looked across the expanse of her garden. "There is no communication like that between the two sides."

Melinda's face was now wet with tears. Augustina tilted her head.

"You must not worry. I feel confident your family knows where you are…certainly Joe has told them."

Melinda's eyes darted up to meet to Augustina's. "Do you know Joe?" she asked in amazement.

Augustina shook her head. "No, I don't, but I do know that he is someone who connects with your thoughts." Augustina held her hand up, allowing a butterfly to land on her finger. The large bright blue insect stayed only an instant before flitting on. "I sense that you are surprised by your own abilities, but you must know that you can feel this person's well-being."

Melinda stared at Augustina before nodding haltingly. "I suppose so. I've known him a long time…but it's always just a lucky guess, isn't it?"

Augustina smiled. "You have a lot to learn about being an Athenite. Since you are from a world that does not recognize our existence, your knowledge about your own people is limited. There are many skills that can be learned. Others are natural to all of us. To know what is on someone's mind is an ancient art form akin to mind reading. Even humans can sometimes accomplish simple forms of it. But yours is a very unique kind that is stronger than simply knowing the thoughts of another. Yours is a deep understanding of a person's entire well-being."

Melinda stared at Augustina, then looked out across the garden. "I think he does know I'm all right…I'm sure I can feel it. I also know he's worried about me, and so is my family. I didn't mean to come here by myself—it just happened. I started to follow the music and then I couldn't stop. Now I just want to go back."

Augustina looked ominous for the first time. "As I have said, I can't help you get back. I will try to locate someone who might help you." She stood up. "You must communicate with your friend, let him know you are all right. Tell him to listen for the music in the air that will bring him and your family to you."

"They know about the music already, because my brother and I deciphered the melodies from some old books. The only problem is that they can't hear it."

"Everyone can hear the sound in the wind. It's like so many things: you have to let your mind relax and believe that you can…and you will." Just then Augustina's son Evan bounded out of the house to join them, and his mother turned to him. "Evan, we are going to help reunite Melinda with her family, but that may take some time. In the meantime, why don't the two of you have some breakfast before you take her on a little tour of the city?"

Breakfast had been simple but surprisingly satisfying. Augustina set the table on the terrace with sparkling dishes and plates piled with sweet rolls and fruit. At first Melinda's appetite was weak, but as the first cup of a rich chocolaty drink was poured, her mouth began watering. She slurped the liquid and bit into an airy pastry. "This is great! I've never tasted anything like it."

Evan eyed his companion. She was obviously enthusiastic about the food; her upper lip sparkled with the sheen of a chocolate mustache, and white icing particles mingled with the freckles that covered her face. When the last sip of her chocolate and the last crumb of her pastry were consumed, he stood up. "If you're finished, let's go."

They left by way of a meandering tour of the house. White marble floors reflected the beauty of exotic furniture in the dining room; oriental carpets and furniture carved of rich dark wood mixed with lighter-colored furnishings adorned the living room. There were all varieties of plants everywhere. Natural light made everything bright and beautiful, shining through dome-shaped windows on every wall. At last they exited through the splendid foyer, with its antique urns and carved wooden tables. Two stone dogs acted as sentries at the front door, the still eyes watching them as they stepped out into the front garden.

The sweet air was warm with only the slightest hint of moisture, giving it the feel of translucent silk. They walked down a long pathway edged with more leafy plants in greens, rusts, and coppers, then out through the tall, black double gates to the street. As they strolled along the avenue, called the Place of the Marquis, Melinda was awestruck by the other estates. Most of the structures were of white stone, with vines covering at least parts of their façades and enormous gardens surrounding the properties.

It was a long walk, at least half an hour, before they reached the town. "This is Tasmay," Evan boasted. "It's the island's biggest city."

"It doesn't look that big," Melinda observed.

"I didn't say it was big, only that it was our biggest. I've studied information about your side of the world. Your cities sound enormous…frighteningly so."

Melinda grimaced. "They're not scary…okay, maybe

just a little. But you get used to them. I've lived all over the world and there are lots of huge cities—Paris, London, New York, Bangkok, Sydney…"

"I know, I know—like I said, I had to learn about them in school. Do you study our side of the world in your schools?"

Melinda laughed and shook her head. "No way!"

Evan looked puzzled. "Why not?"

Melinda stopped walking and looked around. "If you've studied the other side, you know that humans don't know about Athenites, except as characters in storybooks." Her head jerked from side to side, taking in all the magnificent buildings that lined their path. "I hope my parents can find their way here. Mom is a real fan of architecture. That building looks Greek…that one must be Spanish…that is Spanish, isn't it?"

She fascinated Evan. "I suppose so—through the centuries, people have arrived on the island from all over the world. I've never thought about it because everyone is just from Kashdune now."

"Is everyone born here?"

"Not everyone. It doesn't matter, though, because everyone who decides to live here is from here. It is our home, and our loyalty lies with the island."

"That's so weird. Most people I know always refer to where they were born. Like if you were born in one country and move to another, you still consider yourself to be from the country of your birth…oh, never mind, it's not important."

Evan thought about this. "My dad says the other side does have a lot of problems. He said that lots of people don't like each other."

"I suppose." Melinda kept walking, soaking in the beauty of the city. "I think sometimes people don't like the things about each other that are different. It's probably the same here."

Evan shook his head. "Everyone is different here, so everyone is the same. Kashdune is a small place, and we choose to be here. We accept everyone exactly as they are."

"Maybe that's the problem with my side," Melinda mused. "It's really big. There are so many people it makes it difficult to like everyone."

"You don't have to like someone to be able to accept them." Evan smiled, sounding very much like his mother.

Melinda stared at Evan for several steps. He was a few inches shorter than her, and at first glance seemed like any other round-faced, dark-haired ten-year-old boy. It was odd, she thought—she couldn't remember him at all from their first meeting on the beach. She looked away for a second, and even though she had just looked at him, she couldn't produce a picture of him in her mind. His face blended in with the world around him, becoming lost to memory. Now that she thought about it, she couldn't conjure up an image of his mother either. It was as if Augustina didn't exist at all. Her head jerked around to look at Evan again. There was something familiar and yet foreign about him, as if she didn't recognize him at all.

"Do humans accept each other even though they might dislike certain things?"

Melinda sighed. "A lot of humans accept each other, and many like each other. It's the ones who don't that cause the problems. It's really complicated, but that's why over there you can't let humans know about Athenites…at least not right now. If they saw us transform, we'd probably find ourselves locked up in a zoo."

"So why don't you stay here? We're all different and the same; we're mostly Athenite, and life is good. We all try to get along. Besides, you can always go back to visit. My dad does all the time. He told me that when I'm old enough he's going to take me along," Evan said proudly.

Melinda glared at him. "I can't stay here…the other side is *my* home."

They continued their walk in silence until they came to a very busy street with lots of shops and restaurants. Colorful awnings shaded the windows of the buildings and the walkways were crowded with people.

"What's that?" Melinda asked, pointing to a very busy sidewalk café.

"Frozen delight parlor…you must have that on the other side."

Melinda looked puzzled, her mouth fixed in a frown. "Frozen what?"

"Delight." He chuckled. "It's cold, creamy, and sweet…"

"Is it like ice cream?"

"I suppose. It's made from cream and sugar and other stuff. It's kind of frozen but soft just the same." Evan shrugged.

"It *is* ice cream! That's just what I was talking about…it's the same, but because it has a different name some people might not like it."

"That doesn't sound very smart…people wouldn't like something just because of a different name?"

Melinda groaned. "I said it was complicated." She stared at the huge bowls of the creamy dessert on the café tables. "But I'm not bothered by a name. I'd love to try some!"

"Frozen delight" looked the same as ice cream, and even tasted the same. Melinda all but licked her bowl. Since Evan was only halfway through his, she had plenty of time to examine her surroundings. They were in a very lively restaurant, filled with young patrons. She slapped her hand over her sticky mouth to prevent a giggle from escaping as she leaned over to Evan conspiratorially. "Look!" she whispered. "He has donkey ears!" Evan frowned as Melinda continued sniggering, observing the crowd. There were boys with monkey tails and girls with lambs' ears; tiger paws on one young man and another who looked like a cast member from *CATS*. Some kids were covered in fur, some sprouted antlers, and others had shiny black noses or hog-like snouts. "I can't believe this…it's like a fancy dress-up party, only better." She laughed loudly.

Evan scowled at her. "They're teenagers—what'd you expect? When Athenites enter maturity, any stray thought can result in a partial transformation…you should know that. Stop staring, you're being rude."

Melinda looked back and smiled at Evan, controlling her urge to giggle. "You would never see this on the other side—not even from Athenites. When I couldn't control my changes, my family kept me in the house, away from other people."

"So you ran away?" Evan said, now thinking he knew Melinda's secret.

"I didn't run away! My family had to keep my changes under control because humans would freak if they saw this kind of stuff. But Mom and Dad have always believed that Athenites should be able to live like this." The memory of her parents sent a sudden sadness through her, and she pushed her bowl away. "Let's go back. I don't feel so good anymore."

As they walked back toward Evan's house, Melinda stopped suddenly in the middle of the sidewalk. "It's not working. They can't hear the music…they'll never be able to come here!" she cried.

"What's not working?" Evan asked, grabbing her by a shoulder.

"I just got a strong feeling from Joe. They've tried, but they can't hear it. They'll never be able to get to this side. I have to go to them," she whispered through the tears that had begun to creep down her face.

"We'll get my mom—she always knows how to fix things." The two ran down the Place of the Marquis, and before they got to the gates to Evan's house, he called out, "My dad's home! He'll be able to help you!"

"I don't understand, how do you know he's home?"

Evan gave her a disapproving look. "I can feel it. You may be able to transform, but you have a lot to learn about being Athenite. Come on!" Evan took off in the fastest run Melinda had ever seen. She had always considered herself fairly speedy, having been first in every school sports day she'd attended, but Evan ran like lightning.

When she had finally made it into the dining room, he was already out on the terrace explaining everything to his father. Slightly embarrassed at her intrusion, she waited just inside the doorway.

"Slow down," Evan's father said, hugging his son. "It's good to see you too." He turned toward Melinda, motioning for her to join them. "Hello, Melinda. I'm Evan's father. It's nice to meet you. There is someone I'd like you both to meet." He turned to someone just out of Melinda's field of vision. "This is my son Evan and, as you have just heard, this young lady has recently joined us from the other side," he said, motioning toward Melinda. "Evan, Melinda—say hello to a new arrival who has decided to live on Kashdune. His name is Horace Stumpworthy."

CHAPTER EIGHTEEN

Joe stood on the balcony of the Huttons' suite, staring out across the azure water of the sea. He shook his head violently as shivers went up his spine.

"Is Melinda all right?" Felix's quivering voice startled him from behind.

Joe jerked around. "I think so," he answered hesitantly. "To be honest, I don't know what is happening. I've been getting a strong sense that hearing this navigational music is the key to finding her. It's all I've been thinking about. Then, out of the blue, I get this image of Horace Stumpworthy."

"What does that mean?"

Joe looked back out at the water. "I have no idea. I've been concentrating on this connection I seem to have with your sister…trying to find a way to help her. Then in a flash, Horace Stumpworthy arrived in my mind—but not as a rodent. He was human. I haven't given him a thought since his disappearance. Strange…it made me feel anxious, but I'm not concerned about him anymore. I doubt if the little furball is even still alive."

Felix walked to the railing and looked down at the sandy white beach. "Probably just a stray thought, then.

Brain chemistry works in mysterious ways." He paused, watching the rhythm of the waves as they rolled onto the shore. "Following the music may be our only way of finding Melinda. We already know it's the best way of locating Kashdune."

Joe nodded. "That's the hard part. How do we do that?"

Felix turned to go back inside, then stopped. "Melinda can't be the only one able to hear it—surely the journals prove that." He swung back around when he heard splashes in the surf. "What was that?"

"A dolphin." Joe sighed. "I used to transform into them when I was younger…it's a fantastic feeling to sail weightlessly through the sea at incredible speeds."

"Melinda said she wanted to swim with them at the resort…she wanted to become one, actually." Felix folded his arms on top of the rail and leaned forward. Then he straightened up abruptly. "Wait a minute…dolphins can hear one hundred times better than humans!" Then turning toward Joe: "Maybe it's time you dusted off your own dolphin suit and went swimming."

Joe's face screwed up slightly. "Most animals can hear significantly better than humans, but your parents and I have been animals before and none of us have heard the music. And Harmony can use animal senses any time without transforming, and she's never heard it."

"I know, but maybe you just weren't listening for it, since you didn't know it was there," Felix insisted.

"That's what Melinda kept saying…in fact, I think she's been trying to communicate that message since she left." Joe turned to face Felix. "It's true that what you don't know about often doesn't exist in your mind."

"But when you open your mind to other possibilities…"

Elaine agreed with their proposal, at least in principle. She nodded along as Felix explained his dolphin theory and then turned to look out the window at the endless seascape. "It's worth a try. What other options do we have?"

Harmony shook her head. "I know we're all hoping for the best here, but I tried to hear the music in Paris. All I heard was a lot of traffic."

Joe glared at his niece. "If no one has a better suggestion, I think we should try Felix's plan." For an instant his eyes glazed over. "Relax and open your mind. The music is on the winds." He shook his head, blinking wildly. "I've forgotten what I was saying…I feel like I've just stepped out of a trance."

"You were talking about following Felix's plan," Harmony answered. "I suppose it is our only option…for now."

The next day, at eleven in the morning, Joe proudly greeted Harmony, Elaine, Jake, and Felix at the dock of a small marina in the town center. "She's not much to look at," he said, motioning to a boat docked at the end of the long jetty, "but she'll do the trick."

"That's what you spent all that money securing?" Harmony sighed.

"There are no other boats available for hire on this island. The university was our only hope, and they were reluctant to let us *borrow* their marine research vessel until I suggested making a rather sizeable donation to their school." Joe walked briskly toward the vessel, followed by the others, who were considerably less enthusiastic.

"It reminds me of that rusty old moped in Turkey. Are you sure it'll float?" Felix asked, as they got closer to the ancient-looking hulk.

"She's floating now, isn't she?" Joe looked cross. "I checked it out as best I could, and it seems sound. Plus it's big enough to go out past the surf zone and carry all of us safely."

"Let's get moving," said Jake.

Elaine looked nervous, not taking her eyes off the rusty boat bobbing on the water. "Maybe we shouldn't all go… Felix, you should stay here."

Felix swung around, frowning. "Why should I stay? I'm the one who found the music and developed the plan."

"You don't transform. What if that *thing* sinks? Your father, Joe, and I will be dolphins, and Harmony can use her talents to swim like a fish, but what would happen to you?" Elaine said, wringing her hands unconsciously.

Joe looked disappointed. "It's not going to sink, I assure you…well, I don't think it is, anyway. Even if it did, which I'm not saying it will, I have checked the emergency supplies and I'm happy to inform you that it is equipped with state-of-the-art lifeboats, radios, and survival provisions."

"And you don't think it will sink?" Harmony said, squinting at the scuffed word on the side of the hull. "What's the name….*Seenbetredas? Seen-betre-das?* Seen Better Days! You can say that again!"

"This is ridiculous…we can't tell anything from here. Joe's checked it out, but if it'll make you feel more comfortable, check it out for yourselves." Jake began walking purposefully toward the boat. "And Felix *is* going with us, because we need him."

Felix smiled nervously. He wasn't sure if he wanted to set out to sea on the old rust bucket after all, but his father's insistence that he was important to the mission forced him to keep his reservations to himself.

Up close, the boat, with its pattern of rusty streaks and dents, did nothing to reassure Elaine, Harmony, and Felix. Even Jake seemed to hesitate at the thought of going aboard. Joe, however, was eager to get underway. "Come on, you landlubbers…climb aboard," he called over his shoulder as he stepped onto the gangplank.

The vessel tilted as each of them climbed aboard, doing little to calm their fears. The hollow sound of their footsteps on deck seemed to echo loudly as they padded across the bow and along the narrow deck toward the engine room. "Come on, ignore all that," Joe urged, ducking through a metal doorway into the cabin. Smiling devilishly, he welcomed them inside.

"Oh my," Elaine shrieked. Behind her, Harmony gasped. "Who would have thought?"

Even Felix sighed as he carefully stepped in through the threshold. The cabin was very different from the outside appearance: a richly polished room of dark wood paneling, with leatherette sofas and chairs encircling the comfortable living space. "Why didn't you tell us about this before?"

Joe sniggered. "You saw the outside of this boat. Would you have believed me if I told you the inside was rather luxurious? The university keeps it looking like a worthless hunk of tin on the outside to discourage thieves. It has proved to be an excellent deterrent. The boat is actually quite new, as you can see...it's very sound, as well as comfortable. Nothing to worry about."

Elaine smiled painfully. "Except hearing the music."

After two hours of steady cruising through the crystal-clear water, Joe cut the engines, allowing the vessel to drift in the calm sea. He and Harmony had been piloting from the bridge, located up a spiral staircase from the cabin. "Hear anything, Harmony?"

She shook her head solemnly.

"Anything yet?" Felix echoed as he trotted up the stairs, followed closely by his parents. When he saw the expression on their faces, he knew the answer. "Then it's time to unleash the dolphins."

"Exactly what I was thinking," Joe agreed. "We're far enough from shore not be seen. Harmony, you and Felix will have to pilot now. It's actually very easy—ignition is here, speed and direction controls are here, and this big wheel is…"

"Yes, yes—I know, it's all very simple. What exactly are you planning?" Harmony squeezed passed Joe and took her place in the captain's chair.

"We'll transform as soon as we enter the water," Jake answered. "I suggest swimming in wide circles around the boat."

Harmony looked past him, focusing on the glistening reflection off the water. "Melinda kept telling me to open my mind, to accept that the music is real…she said it is everywhere around us."

"That's the feeling I keep getting as well," Joe said.

"This is going to be difficult. We might as well get going." Elaine walked back toward the stairs, motioning for Jake and Joe to join her.

"Relax and believe," Joe said absently, then shook his head, "I'm sorry, I drifted off for a second."

"You said relax and believe," Felix reminded him.

"Probably good advice," Jake observed, following Elaine down the stairs. "Oh," he called over his shoulder, "don't start the engine unless we send you a signal."

"What kind of signal?" Felix asked.

"Good question. Ah…how about one of us leaping into the air?" Joe trotted down the stairs after Jake and Elaine.

Felix followed them down the steps and onto the rear deck. The air was warming up, almost becoming hot, and there was very little in the way of a breeze. Still, he was shivering. "G-g-g-good l-l-l-luck," he stuttered. "I…I have a g-g-good feeling about this."

Jake smiled knowingly. "Me too," he called as he dived off the side of the boat and into the clear water.

Joe and Elaine splashed in to join him, then all three transformed into dolphins. Unlike usual, Felix actually enjoyed the spectacle. It was a far cry from Melinda's pained attempts to change into other creatures. Felix smiled remembering her misshapen bear in Turkey. "I'd love to see how she would mutate into a dolphin," he giggled, before a somber mood took over. "Hang on, Mel—we'll be there soon."

He watched as the three sleek, torpedo-shaped mammals circled the boat. His heart raced with excitement, feeling certain that something extraordinary was about to happen. After about half an hour, their path widened and they traveled farther away from the boat. Slowly and methodically they pursued the elusive sound they prayed would guide them to Melinda.

Felix left the back of the boat for the bow. Four rusty benches were anchored to the deck, each facing outward. They weren't terribly comfortable, but they gave him a good vantage point from which to watch the team's progress in the water. The sea remained calm with only small, gently rolling swells to sway the boat. Time passed slowly, and he closed his eyes and listened for the music. The subtle rippling of water against the hull was the only thing he heard. His head swayed with the bobbing of the vessel. It was a hypnotic feeling, with the warm air from above and the rhythmic pulse of the ocean beneath him. His thoughts drifted into the memory of the music Melinda brought alive—the lovely and exotic melodies of Kashdune.

Felix jerked upright, startled by something he couldn't identify. The light was blinding and he had the worst neck-ache of his life. A glance at his watch told him that two hours had elapsed since he sat down. It was now late in the afternoon and he was alone. Springing to his feet, he looked first up at the bridge. Harmony was still in the captain's chair, apparently asleep. "I must have fallen asleep, too," he cried as he looked across the water for a sign of the others. They weren't there. "Mom! Dad! Joe!" he shouted over and over.

A loud splash sounded from the back of the boat. He ran to investigate. When he arrived on the stern there was nothing to see—still no sign of the others and no clue to the disturbance that had woken him. His heart was pounding violently and his breath was coming in desperate gulps. Then, in the distance, he saw a dolphin erupt from the sea. "Harmony! The signal! Start the engines!" he yelled, running back to the cabin.

By the time he sprang up the stairs to the bridge, Harmony was already on the case.

Felix was giddy. "They're back there," he said, pointing. "They must have heard it!"

At full throttle, it only took seconds to reach the dolphins. Harmony's expression melted into a fearful scowl. "Felix, they haven't heard anything…there's a shark!" she shouted, pointing to a massive fin sticking out just above the water. "It looks like a tiger shark; they're huge and extremely deadly!" Harmony steered the boat toward the shark, but it easily avoided the boat, diving and swerving to dodge them.

Felix turned a ghostly white. "We've got to do something!"

Harmony didn't answer at first, feeling uncharacteristically helpless. "Felix, dolphins have been known to kill sharks, and this shark is outnumbered…let's just hope it doesn't have any friends," she said, wishing she hadn't.

"They've got to get out of the water and into the boat! Steer closer to them!" Felix yelled, running down the stairs.

"Felix! Where are you going?"

"There must be something on this ship that will help us—a spear gun or something." He leapt off the steps into the cabin and began searching for anything that might help.

Harmony did her best to interfere with the shark's plans, driving a wild course between it and its dolphin victims. But the huge beast was not dissuaded. It pursued them one after the other while the dolphins, working as a team, defended themselves viciously. Harmony watched in horror and admiration as one of the dolphins rushed straight at the shark. The predator prepared to meet this challenge, but in its eagerness, it failed to notice another dolphin attacking from the side. The shark lashed back with incredible speed, biting at one of them while the other two mounted a combined attack on opposite sides of the beast. The shark twisted madly as blood gushed out of its mouth and gills. The dolphins were working as one, gaining the upper hand as they repeatedly battered the shark.

The once transparent blue water had turned a grisly red. The sickening contest was over. The shark was dead, and its lifeless body sank unceremoniously into the depths of the sea.

Joe, Jake and Elaine swam slowly toward the boat, a streak of red trailing after them. At first Felix assumed it was simply a bit of the shark's blood caught in their current. But it wasn't. One of them was injured, and he knew in his heart which one it was. "Dad's been bitten! Hurry—we've got to help him!"

After pulling the boat closer, Harmony leapt down the steps to help. "You've got to transform or we can't help you up," she called urgently. The three dolphins, with their permanent smiles, looked happy and excited, something that changed dramatically as they shifted back into humans.

"Help Jake up first," Elaine cried. Felix stared at his father's anguished expression and ashen complexion, his eyes fixed on the blood spewing out around him.

"Felix, grab those towels," Harmony barked, pointing to the stack they'd left on one of the benches, while she maneuvered down the ladder to help Jake up onto the deck. "We've got to get him wrapped up…he's slipping into shock, and we've got to stop the bleeding!"

They wrapped Jake in the three towels, leaving Elaine and Joe scrambling to dry off with their clothes. Harmony tried to minimize the shock Jake was rapidly falling into by applying pressure to the wounds on his legs. Within seconds the white towels were soaked in his blood.

"Well, at least I didn't provide that old fellow's last meal…it looks I was just a little appetizer." Jake smiled weakly as his voice quivered. "Help me dress these wounds, then we've got to keep going."

"We've got to get you to a hospital!" Elaine cried.

"I'm a doctor, and perfectly capable of prescribing my own treatment." He winced. "If we go back we'll lose more time, and time is something we haven't got a lot of. We're on the right track now." Jake looked at Felix, smiling proudly. "You were right...*again!* Before we saw that shark I know I heard the music. That means we can do it." He panted painfully, then turning to the others: "How about it, did you hear anything?"

Joe and Elaine, both with wide-eyed expressions, shook their heads. There was a brief flirtation with the thought of success that faded immediately as Jake turned a ghastly grayish color and sank into unconsciousness.

CHAPTER NINETEEN

"Who...is...it?" Melinda called shakily to whoever was tapping at her door.

"It's Evan. You can come out...he's gone to work with my dad."

"What do you mean? Who's gone?" she snapped.

"Horace Stumpworthy. I know you don't want to see him."

Melinda frowned at Evan's suggestion, even though he was absolutely correct. She had been avoiding Professor Stumpworthy since setting eyes on him two days ago, but she didn't like the idea that anyone knew.

It had been horrifying seeing the professor again. Not at first, of course, since she had grown used to seeing Felix transformed into his image. Even when Evan's father, Fredrick Hamsong, introduced him, she was startled but not frightened. That is until she looked into his eyes and recognized him as the real Professor Horace Stumpworthy. That was when terror struck. Her legs wobbled and her stomach rumbled in preparation for ejecting all that lovely ice cream she had eaten earlier.

Luckily Augustina was close by. As Melinda looked like she might collapse, vomit, and scream all at once, Augustina stepped closer. It was as if Augustina had transferred strength into her. Instantly Melinda regained enough composure to confront the professor.

"Melinda Hutton," the professor had greeted her smoothly. "You and I have a bit of a difficult history. I hope that you will accept my apologies for all that transpired between us last time."

Melinda had only stared at him in reply. Her mind raced back to the time when Horace Stumpworthy had betrayed her family and tried to destroy their lives.

"I'm sorry that I wasn't able to greet you properly the last time we met—lemmings have such a limited range of expression," he continued. "Luckily, my dear friend Fredrick rescued me from my sad fate."

Melinda's mouth dropped open in disbelief. "I thought you were supposed to be a lemming forever."

Stumpworthy laughed. "Thankfully not. Fredrick introduced me to a marvelous medicine that cured that condition." He patted Hamsong on the shoulder, then turned back to face Melinda. "My dear, I know that you find this difficult to believe, but being trapped in the body of a helpless animal can change a person. The time I spent in that little cage gave me ample opportunity to re-examine my life. Now that the ordeal is over, I have learned to be thankful for so many things I had taken for granted before. And of course, I owe a debt of gratitude to you and your family for putting me in that position in the first place."

"You're lying!" Melinda yelled, drawing back from him. "You're not the kind of person to be grateful for anything!"

A look of genuine hurt passed over Stumpworthy's face. "I'm afraid that may indeed once have been my nature. But I'm a changed man—surely my friends can assure you of that." He glanced over her head at the Hamsongs, and suddenly Melinda felt a warm hand on her shoulder. She looked up into Augustina's warm eyes.

"People *can* change," Augustina said. "You know that I can read thoughts. Horace has not hidden who he once was from us, and I don't believe he's hiding anything from me now."

Fredrick Hamsong stepped over to Horace's side. "My wife has many amazing gifts; completely knowing the soul of another person is only one of them. Horace knows that we do not condone what he has done, but we must look toward the future and not be buried by the bitter past."

Melinda didn't know what to say, and so said nothing. Could it be possible that Stumpworthy was telling the truth? The Hamsongs seemed to believe that about him, but everything in her screamed to get away. The magical strength Augustina had leant her was enough to make it to her room with her head held high—then of course it had dissolved completely, and she had galloped to the bathroom, knelt in front of the toilet, and hurled the entire contents of her stomach down the toilet.

Melinda shook off the memory of that day and cracked open the door. "I don't know what you're talking about," she announced as soon as she saw that Evan was alone.

Evan frowned. "Mom says you're frightened of him, but she doesn't know why—and that's really strange, because my mother knows everything."

Melinda rolled her eyes and walked across her room toward the door leading to the garden. "All mothers know everything...at least, that's what they like us to think."

Evan laughed. "True. But the ones that can read minds really do know a lot."

Melinda spun around. "Are you serious?"

"Of course I am," he barked. "Don't tell me: people on the other side don't understand telepathy, either! It sounds really backward over there...I'm glad I live here."

"Hmm." Melinda looked down at her bare feet. When she looked up at Evan's smiling face, a lot of things were beginning to make sense. "That's why your mother knows exactly how I'm feeling." She turned away and moved into the sunlit garden. "My mother seems to know what

I'm thinking or feeling, but that's because she's my mom and knows me. But your mother—she really seems to know what's on my mind." She spun around and looked questioningly at Evan. "Can your mom really tell exactly what I'm thinking?"

Evan nodded. "It's not that unusual; most Athenites practice telepathy. I've even heard that some humans can, too…but not as well."

"There you are! Evan, you're late for school," Augustina called as she stepped into the garden from the dining room. She motioned for Evan to be on his way and then turned her smiling face toward Melinda. "How are *you* feeling?"

"Fine, thank you," Melinda answered formally.

"She's worried about you reading her mind," Evan called over his shoulder as he bounded back into the house.

"I told you about mind reading when we first met. You mustn't be worried…I don't make a habit of invading people's thoughts. My use of this talent is only to help others."

Melinda smiled weakly. "Can you read everyone's thoughts?"

Augustina smiled and nodded. "Yes, but to tell you the truth most people's thoughts aren't very interesting. You'd be surprised how some people use their brain energy—it's not very impressive. I tend to feel first, read later."

"I don't understand."

"If I sense that someone is distressed, I may look into their mind to see if I can help."

"Like the other day," Melinda said, looking up shyly.

Augustina grinned wisely. "Everyone has the ability to sense things. We know when someone is approaching or looking at us, and we can sense how people are feeling. We know if someone is sad, happy, or scared without having to hear them say so, or without listening to their thoughts." She motioned for Melinda to join her as she strolled around the garden.

"I suppose it's better sometimes, because it's difficult to put some feelings into words," Melinda sighed. "Like with the professor…I guess I'm glad you know how I feel because I don't want to talk about it."

"I respect that, and I also respect you. I will not say anything else to anyone. I must confess, I told Evan that I didn't think you were fond of Horace. I promise I'll say no more." Augustina took hold of a long-stemmed pink flower. "Isn't this a beautiful color? It reminds me of the beginning of a sunset, before the oranges and reds invade the horizon, when everything is quiet and pink."

Melinda leaned over and sniffed the huge blossom. "It has a nice smell too," she observed.

Augustina nodded. "You know, I was just thinking that very same thing."

Melinda smiled. "Maybe I read your mind!"

"Maybe you did…after all, you have the ability to do so. Evan is learning the basics at school, and I'm teaching him the rest. You would be wise to watch what you're thinking around him…unlike his music lessons, he loves to practice telepathy."

"I like transforming more than I liked my music lessons," Melinda admitted.

Augustina laughed and looked up into the sky. "It's only a few hours until Evan's school lets out." She turned back and met Melinda's eyes. "Why don't you walk down and escort him home today? He enjoys your company."

Melinda smiled guiltily. "I'm not really used to having close friends…we've moved so much that I really don't know how to be friends with anyone."

Augustina smiled. "Well, now might be the perfect time to learn how to do that. Evan makes a very good friend."

Later that afternoon, Melinda made her way out of the house and headed down the Place of the Marquis, following her hostess's directions. Augustina had said the school was only fifteen minutes away.

The street was quiet, with the distant sound of children playing the only disturbance. The last time Melinda had walked this way was when Evan had taken her for ice cream. She snorted, trying to suppress a laugh when she remembered the girl with donkey ears making goo-goo eyes at the boy with monkey hands, his long tail curling around the back of his chair. Evan had been annoyed that she gawked at the teenagers in the café. *But it was so funny*, she thought, laughing out loud. She stopped and then squeezed her eyes shut for a moment, reaching up to touch the top of her head. Her smile widened when her fingers met the hard, bony antlers that had sprung up out of her hair. *This is so cool*, she thought as she proudly strutted down the lane. *You don't have to pretend to be something you're not around here!*

The sound of children's voices was growing louder as she got closer to the school. The sidewalk would soon be swarming with Evan and his classmates. Melinda began to walk more slowly, suddenly feeling very foolish and conspicuous. Again she touched her antlers, but this time with panic instead of joy. *You can do this here*, she reminded herself, trying to calm her nerves. *You're free to be anything you want to be.*

Her stomach fluttered and her face burned with embarrassment when she spotted Evan walking toward her. She grabbed hold of her antlers, closed her eyes, and willed them away.

Evan laughed as he approached. "What made you think about antlers?"

Melinda's face burnt red. "I don't know," she said as she touched the top of her head.

"Don't worry, they're gone. I don't know why you care if

they are or not anyway…nobody would even notice around here."

Melinda shrugged and bit her lip. "It's really nice that people don't care, but I guess I still do. I'm not used to Athenites being so open."

They walked several steps in silence and then Evan stopped. "Hey, do you want to go to the beach to watch some surfing?"

Melinda shook her head. "Your mother is expecting us back."

"She won't mind. I know she'd encourage you to explore the island some more. If you want to go, I'll let her know."

Melinda nodded slowly, half expecting Evan to whip out his cell phone. Instead he closed his eyes and seemed to concentrate for a few seconds, then opened them with a smile. "She says it's okay," he said to Melinda's open-mouth stare.

"I forgot that you could do that," she sighed.

"Do what?"

"Telepathy."

"You can too," Evan encouraged. "It's really easy when you get the hang of it. You should be able to at least send thoughts to other people. The difficult part is sending your thoughts to someone who doesn't know how to communicate that way…sometimes they think that *your* thoughts are actually *theirs*."

The beach was on the other side of Tasmay. They walked to the end of the Place of the Marquis and then down a long, sandy path lined with tall palms, wild purple orchids, banana trees, and fragrant gardenias. At the end of the path was a wide beach of sparkling white sand, all of it crowded with young Athenites.

Evan looked at Melinda, who had lifted a hand to her mouth. "Don't stare," he warned her. "It's not like you haven't seen this before."

Melinda nodded, her eyes twinkling with delight at the scene in front of her. There must have been at least fifty people there, all sporting some sort of animal appendage—dog paws, lamb tails, seal flippers, and one girl with a feathered crown on her head like a colorful cockatoo. Melinda tried to suppress a giggle, but it just came out as a snort instead.

"I thought you said there was surfing," she managed through her laughter. "I don't see any surfboards."

Evan rolled his eyes. "We don't need surfboards," he said as he pointed toward the waves.

Melinda saw them immediately. They were hard to miss: three sleek dolphins surfing toward the shore, their dorsal fins above the water glinting in the sunshine. When they reached the sand, their tails instantly changed into two human legs, while human arms and hands replaced their flippers. Once out of the surf zone, each dolphin's head transformed into that of a human, leaving two boys and a girl, each of them half human but still half dolphin in the middle.

"Why don't they change all the way?" Melinda wondered aloud.

"Why bother?" Evan shrugged. "They're probably going back out after those three." He gestured to three girls, more dolphin than human, running toward the water. They trotted down the beach on their human legs and then splashed into the surf. As soon as water was above their knees they dove in, transforming instantly. Their legs disappeared into tails, their arms widened then flattened into flippers, and human heads morphed into those of dolphins.

Melinda gasped. "That is so cool!"

Evan smiled. "You don't find it so funny anymore?"

She couldn't take her eyes off of the dolphins effortlessly surfing in with the waves. "It's amazing," she breathed, looking around at the beach.

"It's not really amazing. It's just the way it is here. It's natural."

"I wish it was like this on the other side," Melinda said sadly.

Evan smiled. "That's why we live here. We can be free on Kashdune. You could be too."

The *Nautica* drifted in the flat sea, having just returned from the violent currents of the access. "I haven't done that for a very long time," Fredrick panted, sweat glistened on his face, "…going back into the access so soon. It's dangerous to overdo exposure to the cloud; it can be very disorienting. I think we'll be all right as long as we don't go back in for at least a couple of weeks," Fredrick called to Horace across the bow of the boat, where he was organizing the equipment they had used in their experiments. "I hope the cloud samples we collected will be sufficient." He checked to make sure that all of the fifty test tubes were secured inside their case.

Horace nodded. "We'll have enough to keep us busy. I suspect we'll only need one or two of the samples to determine the makeup of the cloud. I can tell already that the mist contains a lot more than water vapor. There are a lot of chemicals mingling in that fog." Stumpworthy checked the line that held the anchor and then walked toward the cabin. "Once the composition is determined, we can start testing methods to alter the density and influence the way it carries sound. If we're successful, which I'm quite certain we will be, we should be able to alter the musical impulses that filter through. Anyone following the melody that currently exists will be forced off course. Where exactly they end up is anybody's guess."

Fredrick Hamsong smiled awkwardly. "We have debated the issue for centuries. Now we all agree: regardless of the consequences, we will feel much better to be safely tucked away from harm."

"I still don't understand your paranoia. Who are you afraid of?"

Fredrick lifted the two cases that held the test tubes and followed Horace toward the cabin. "Most people on the other side view Kashdune, our people, and our resources as the thing of fairy tales. It wasn't always that way. There have been times in history when people knew of our existence and carried out great expeditions to find us. Most ended in failure. As the centuries passed, fewer people believed in our existence, resulting in fewer and fewer intruders. However, many still come by accident when they follow the music—the siren's song that leads to Kashdune. Humans call the access the Bermuda Triangle because of the mysterious disappearances of boats and planes. Many of those who vanished are still here today, thanks to the same water that you and I are now dependent on."

"The water…you mean the medicine that saved me?"

"The water is more powerful than any medicine on Earth. It is the magic elixir of youth and health. For an Athenite, it brings immortality. For a human, it is the cure for almost anything. Centuries ago, explorers searched for the Fountain of Youth, but only a few actually found it. Me, for one."

Horace paused briefly, wondering just how old his old friend really was. "So if no one knows about the access and the island, let alone the water, what are you worried about?"

"Nothing can stay as it has been. The world changes. There are people who think only of themselves or their causes. They think nothing of destroying others." Horace held the door of the cabin open and Fredrick stepped through. "A few years ago, we had a visitor—an Athenite, as it happens. He took up residence on the island, travelling back to the other side from time to time. He turned out to be an unscrupulous individual who had plans to use the water and the seclusion of Kashdune for his organization. He was connected to people whose extreme beliefs threatened entire populations. Their use of violence and extortion to manipulate the world was growing at a frightening speed.

He believed he could use our world as the headquarters from which their terrifying group of anarchists, thugs, and murderers could safely operate for all time."

"He obviously failed."

"Only by luck. He was killed in a motorcycle accident on the other side, apparently while trying to escape the police. But soon after the incident, our citizens decided that we needed to protect our world from…well…ah…*yours.*"

Horace climbed the stairs that led to the bridge, followed by Fredrick. He sat in the captain's chair while Fredrick reclined in the passenger's seat. Both remained quiet until Stumpworthy started the engine and slowly brought the boat into a smooth acceleration that cut cleanly through the glassy water. Horace looked concerned and thoughtful, his mind racing with all the information now at his disposal. "My guess is that it shouldn't take long to alter the cloud. I'm quite confident we'll be able to change things for the better. By the way…what about the girl, Melinda? Are you going to take her back to the other side?"

Fredrick shook his head. "I'll be unable to make the trip for a long time, and I can't instruct her about the music. It's very dangerous, and I wouldn't feel right about sending a child through from this side all alone. Her only hope is that her family comes for her."

Stumpworthy shook his head. "They may not make it in time, if the access changes sooner than expected."

Fredrick nodded. "Let us pray they *do* make it through."

"Of course, my friend." Stumpworthy nodded. "I dread to think what fate awaits them otherwise…"

CHAPTER TWENTY

Jake was enjoying his journey through a musical mist. A magical, indescribable melody pulled him across a glistening sea and into a cottony vapor that rested on the horizon. The creamy ivory cloud surrounded him, calming his spirit as it cradled his body. He didn't know if he was standing, sitting, or perhaps even lying down. Whatever position he assumed didn't seem to matter as he floated, carried by an invisible force toward the enchanting music. In the distance, a woman's voice beckoned, "You can hear the music, Jake...you must follow it."

"Sirens," he laughed. "The sirens of the sea!" He wanted to follow the captivating melody, but could he trust the song? The image of a woman was almost visible in the distance, disguised by the mist. Her long, dark hair wafted around her head, obscuring her face.

"Follow the music," she sang again and again. He smiled and shook his head, confident that he could resist her.

"Jake...Jake," she commanded in a very different tone. "Come on, Jake."

He laughed, shaking his head slowly. "I need to find Melinda...maybe you can help me," he called back.

"Elaine and Felix have gone to find her...you must

stay with us and rest a while," she barked. Her voice had become harsh and raspy.

"How do you know them…how do you know where they've gone?"

"They were here, but they've gone to find Melinda. They said they'll be back soon, and you're not to worry."

Her voice had lost its melodious quality. He could no longer see her; the cloud had disappeared and everything had become dark. He chuckled to himself. "Of course I can't see anything—my eyes are closed," he sighed, feeling quite the fool. But when he opened them, the blinding brightness of the light, let alone the sight of the woman leaning over him, was dreadful. A very large woman with a broad face, flushed pink cheeks, and a bulbous red nose that held up perfectly round spectacles glared down at him. There was definitely no music surrounding this lady.

"Dr. Hutton, you're fine now, nothing to worry about. We've got the fever under control, and everything else is healing nicely," said the rotund woman, smiling.

Almost dizzy with the reality of the situation, Jake realized he was flat on his back, resting uncomfortably on a hard mattress. As his eyes regained their focus, he also noted where he was—and it wasn't floating across the sea on a magic cloud. A brief scan of the room identified it as a clinically decorated hospital room. He closed his eyes and willed himself to return to the other world of music and sirens.

"Your wife will be back as soon as she can, but now you must rest." Again he opened his eyes and struggled to focus on the blurred face in front of him. "Don't worry, Dr. Hutton. You're in good hands. Though we were all a bit worried. When your wife brought you in, it looked like you might not make it."

"Where am I?" Jake managed in a croaky voice.

"All Saints Hospital. We don't have very many shark

attacks here, but there's always the possibility. You're very lucky to be alive."

"How long have I been here? Where are my wife and son?"

"You've been here for three days," said the woman, whom Jake now recognized as a nurse. "Your wife said she'd be back in a few days. Poor dear, with your daughter gone she was torn in two about where she was most needed. After we knew you were out of danger, she and your son left to collect your daughter. That was two days ago."

"They've only lost a couple of days," Jake moaned softly.

"There's not been a lot to miss, as you've been asleep," chuckled the incessantly jolly nurse.

Jake sighed, realizing that to explain anything would be fruitless. He closed his eyes and willed his strength back into his limbs, shuddering at the thought of his injury. He remembered it now—the shark grabbing him like a toy, throwing his body around as if he were a rag doll and ripping into his flesh. He remembered the searing pain down his tail and the relief he had felt when the shark released him.

He reached up with his right hand and rubbed his face, then tried to shift to a more comfortable position. When he tried to move his legs, only one responded; he had no feeling in the other. He lay back, exhausted from the slight exertion and nervous about what he might find under the covers—or more to the point, what he wouldn't find.

"It'll be okay," the nurse assured him, just a little too cheerfully. "A lot of people function without one. It'll take getting used to, but you'll be all right."

"Is it all gone?" Jake tried to steady his voice.

"I'm afraid it is," the nurse bubbled. "My granny lost hers in an accident years ago; hobbles a bit when she walks, but it's no big deal"

Jake thought he might vomit. He squeezed his eyes shut to shove the feeling down.

"Dr. Hutton, you of all people should know that it's

not the end of the world," the nurse chirped.

Jake glowered at the smiling woman who seemed to be enjoying his predicament. "Maybe not the end of the world, but I certainly wouldn't make light of it. A leg is a terrible thing to lose," he growled.

The nurse frowned for the first time, then burst into a hearty and, in Jake's mind, sadistic laugh. She threw the covers back and exposed his bandaged appendage. "You silly man—you've only lost your big toe! The rest of it is still there, under all these bandages. The only danger you were in was the fact that you almost bled to death, and you developed a rather nasty infection. I'm happy to tell you that you are recovering nicely. You're just going to be very weak for a while."

Still chuckling heartily, the nurse left the room. Jake slumped back in the bed as relief sucked away what little strength he had. Gradually sleep overtook him, and to his great joy he was reunited with the magic of a sparkling sea and its intoxicating music.

Far out at sea, Felix drifted in and out of sleep on the deck of the marine research vessel. Three days ago, after leaving his father in the hospital, he, his mother, Joe, and Harmony had set out again, hoping to locate the music that would lead them to Melinda. It was a painfully boring process. Each day he took up his position on one of the benches in the bow of the boat. Joe and Elaine, transformed once again into dolphins, swam in increasingly larger circles around the vessel. Hours passed with nothing to do but watch the rippling sea and catch an occasional glimpse of the two dolphins as they skimmed the surface.

"Hear anything?" Harmony asked, startling him awake.

Felix shrugged. "I hear lots of things…even music."

He paused, but just for an instant, not wanting to get Harmony too excited. "In my mind, though, not in the air," he sighed.

"Maybe you *are* hearing it properly…after all, your memory can't replay something you haven't experienced."

"True—but remember, I'm linked with my dad in the same way Joe is connected to Melinda. I think I'm hearing his memories of the music. At first I thought I might be hearing the song, but it was too dreamlike. I figure now that Dad is recovering, he's probably thinking a lot about the music, especially since he's just lying in bed with nothing else to do. And because I've been thinking a lot about him, I'm connecting to his thoughts." Felix leaned forward and stared out at the sea. "I take it Mom and Joe haven't heard it either?"

Harmony shook her head. "I've been awake the entire time they've been in the water, and there's been no sign." She crossed to the railing, searching the smooth swells. "Your father will be able to leave the hospital soon, and then he can lead us to…wait a minute. Look over there." Harmony pointed at the horizon, where a dolphin had leapt free of the water. "It must be your mother or Joe, I haven't seen any other dolphins around here." Suddenly animated, she turned and ran for the bridge, yelling, "Please God, not another shark!"

Harmony raced across the deck with Felix at her heels. As Harmony fumbled with the ignition, Felix watched the activity in the sea with horror. "Hurry!" he screamed. "Now they're both leaping up!"

The vessel churned through the water at top speed, but since they were a considerable distance from the dolphins, it took a painfully long time to get there. "The sea is turning a bit choppy," Harmony called as the boat splashed through an increasingly rough sea. "It looks stormy up ahead—hang on and keep your wits about you, because it's going to be a bumpy ride."

"Where did this come from?" Felix yelled back.

"Looks like some kind of freak storm. As soon as we pick up your mother and Joe, we'll turn back. This is not the kind of sea I'm comfortable sailing through." The boat pitched violently as waves grew to several meters in height.

"Slow down…there they are!" Felix ran back down the stairs and ricocheted off the banister as he clumsily made his way to the deck.

"Hang on to something that's bolted down," called Harmony, following him shakily down the spiral steps. "We're okay for the moment, but we've got to get out of here before this storm heats up even more."

The dolphins stopped leaping about and surfaced with just their heads bobbing above the waves. Both chattered in unison as Felix positioned the ladder over the side. "Get on board and let's get out of here!"

"Felix! They said they found the music! They both heard it, and they want us to follow," Harmony shrieked over the howling wind and sound of waves smacking against the hull.

"We should go back and wait the storm out," Felix protested.

Harmony translated his concern to the others, and then shook her head. "They say the sea is a lot calmer up ahead."

Felix wasn't so sure, as he looked across the dark, stormy ocean, but he had little opportunity to object as the dolphins leapt free of the water, spinning away from the boat.

"Come on, we've got to keep up with them," Harmony shouted. She maneuvered back up the steps, feeling very much like a pinball as she bounced against the walls and furnishings. Felix's complexion was now taking on a greenish hue, while his stomach was doing such a flip-flopping tango, as he crawled up behind Harmony, that he was very nearly sick.

Harmony gently pushed on the throttle, slowly accelerating the boat. It pitched violently through the waves, which were not levelling out—in fact, they were only getting higher. Torrents of water sloshed over the bow as the boat surfed down each crest and then slashed through the waves in the trough.

"We can't keep going into this," Felix screamed. "This boat will be ripped to shreds!" At the exact instant the words escaped his lips, the water suddenly stilled. "This can't be real," he gasped, staring at the water that was now smooth as glass. Harmony stood beside him open-mouthed, her expression proving that she didn't understand it either. When Felix looked back at the sea behind them, where the storm should have been, he saw nothing but gorgeous, glistening, calm blue water all the way to the horizon. "This is too weird," he whispered.

Harmony gulped, fighting down her fear. "Keep watching Joe and Elaine," she said in a jittery voice. "A strange fog is picking up. It's like the storm. It wasn't there a minute ago, but it certainly is now. Don't lose sight of them!" As her words faded, so did the blue sky and brilliant sunshine, replaced at once by a white mist thick as cotton.

"What's happening now?" Felix yelled as the boat moved into the vapor—but it was like yelling into a pillow. He could barely hear his own voice. He looked at Harmony, who was talking at the same time, but he couldn't hear what she was saying either. The cloud was thickening by the second, absorbing everything; even the roar of the boat's engine was muffled into a soundless vibration.

Harmony switched off the engine for fear of heading in the wrong direction as the cloud thickened. The absence of the vibration only made the experience more surreal.

Felix searched the sea for signs of his mother and Joe, but this monster cloud had consumed everything, including the sea itself, as it gobbled up the world, or at least concealed everything inside its moist white shroud. Panicking, he looked for some kind of sign from Harmony, but she too had vanished into the mist. All around him was white—there were no shapes, no colors, only the impenetrable thickness of the dense cloud that had erased everything.

Elaine and Joe swam on, quite oblivious to the diminished visibility. The music grew in strength, drawing them deeper into its hypnotic power. It was a pleasant feeling, even though their thoughts became muddled and all other desires were replaced with an insatiable appetite for the next piece of the melody. They glided effortlessly through the water, pulled by a magnetic force that only few could resist. Elaine was about to become one of the few.

As Joe swam independently onward through the mist, Elaine was hit with a familiar instinct she'd felt hundreds of times before: her son was in trouble. "Felix!" she called to no avail. Dolphins could communicate from great distances; her call should have carried for miles, but the cloud was like a vacuum. Within it there was room for only one sound: the music that penetrated the depths of the ocean and clung to the impenetrable mist.

Elaine floated eerily in a sea with no current or swell. It was like being in a stagnant and lifeless pond, yet held in the grip of a force so powerful that it laid claim to everything in its domain. The music was trying to take ownership of her, too. But motherhood was an even stronger pull, and with one supreme effort she threw off the music and willed her body to do as *she* commanded.

Felix was cold, but sweating profusely. It was hard to relax surrounded by the cottony fog. He called out several times, but couldn't make even a squeak. *If I can't hear myself, then no one else can either.* His mind raced. *I've got to stay calm… think, Felix, think!* He tried taking a step, but it felt like he was stepping into nothingness, a nauseating sensation that permeated his head and stomach. *I've got to think of something else. How can I attract attention? No one can see us or hear us, but they could feel us…*He bit his lip. *Sea animals react to vibration— but without the engine on, we'll have little of that. I've got to create a disturbance that will send out that kind of signal.* He began marching in place, feeling terribly off balance with every stomp. It was the strangest thing he had ever done. He couldn't hear his own footsteps and he certainly couldn't see his limbs moving. Only the pressure on the soles of his feet confirmed that he was indeed doing anything.

Elaine's heart pounded when she heard a faint vibration travelling through the water. *That must be them—but it's so faint I can't tell which direction I need to swim. There's only one thing that can help me find something that can't be seen or heard. I've got to use sonar, and a whale is my best bet.*

She froze her movements and concentrated, losing herself in the sensation of change. Her sleek body grew to a hundred times its original size as she slowly evolved into the massive form of a great blue whale. Focusing in the direction of the minute vibrations, she sent out sonar waves from the crown of her head. Within seconds the waves bounced back to her. *Straight ahead,* she thought, relieved. *Please be them and not some nasty, harpoon-wielding whaler.*

It only took a few minutes to reach a boat. Slowly cruising around the hull, she continued to send out signals that she hoped would differentiate the bow from the stern. *I don't know if this is right, but let's give it a go,* she thought as she bumped her nose against what she hoped was the stern. *Okay, folks, let's get this thing moving…and please don't turn on the propeller.* She pumped her tail with smooth and elegant power and began pushing the boat toward the music.

Felix, still stomping like a drum major in a marching band, fell to the floor as the boat surged forward. It was extremely disorienting to be rolling across the white abyss. More than once he attempted to stand, but each time the bobbing and swaying of the boat, coupled with his feeling of vertigo, sent him crashing back to the floor. The whole experience was nauseating. Finally, curled in a tight little ball, he closed his eyes. *I've got to come up with another plan*, he thought desperately.

A few minutes passed with Felix in this prone position before he heard the faint sound of a voice. "It's gone," Harmony wheezed. "Are you all right?"

"Harmony?" Felix croaked, his voice sounding strangely unfamiliar. He opened his eyes to colors and shapes, golden sunlight filtering into the bridge. He uncoiled and carefully stood up. "That was a weirdest thing I've ever been through."

"I must admit it comes close. It was certainly unpleasant." Harmony jerked her head to look out the side porthole. Then she gasped. "I don't know how we're doing it, but were moving. The engine is switched off, and I'm certainly not driving. Maybe the current is taking us."

Felix darted over to the window. "Are you sure the engine isn't running?" he asked.

She shook her head. "I haven't touched the ignition since turning it off in that cloud."

"Well, something is propelling us, because there aren't any currents out there. I can't see anything pulling from the bow."

"Take a look at the stern—perhaps we're being pushed," Harmony suggested.

Felix cautiously maneuvered to the rear of the cabin to check it out. He gaped at the ocean behind them. "A whale!" he cried.

Harmony laughed, joining him at his vantage point. "Are you acquainted with any big blue whales?"

For the first time in hours Felix's worry was replaced with relief. "It's probably my mom…she's always been a bit on the pushy side."

CHAPTER TWENTY-ONE

Melinda woke up for the sixteenth time. There wasn't a breeze to cool the warm, humid air and no pleasant chirp of insects to ease the swirling thoughts that kept her from relaxing into a deep sleep. She was lying on top of her covers, having never ventured beneath them since lying down several hours ago. The dawn was marking its arrival with faint rays of bronze light, and the air was already filled with birdsong. She sighed as her agitation festered.

She rolled over, struggling to go back to sleep when Horace Stumpworthy burst into her mind. The mere fact that he was living on Kashdune was unsettling, let alone the fact that he seemed to be good friends with Fredrick Hamsong. Luckily he hadn't remained at the Hamsong house, instead taking up residence on his yacht in the harbor. Even so, he was rarely out of her thoughts. Evan told her that Stumpworthy was working on an important project with his father; the two of them spent hours together, travelling out to sea or working in his father's laboratory with another man named Albert Easton. Melinda was convinced that the three of them must be up to something sinister.

She slithered out of bed and padded across the cool floor and through the door out to the garden. "I can't stay here without my family," she whimpered. Then she closed her eyes and transformed into a kestrel, flapping her wings silently as she escaped into the predawn sky.

Augustina materialized across the garden, tilting her face up to watch Melinda's flight. She smiled kindly and spoke in a whisper, blowing a kiss into the wind. "Be careful, my precious one. Slow down and listen—watch the world around you and understand what you are hearing."

Evan plodded sleepily across the dew-soaked grass to his mother's side. "Did Melinda leave?"

She nodded. "I'm proud of you. You're learning to connect with the things around you."

"I felt her frustration and her movements…they woke me up," he slurred in a yawn. "Will she come back?"

"I believe she will, darling. She still has so much to learn. What she seeks is within reach if she slows down and listens to the thoughts already circulating in her mind."

Melinda flew low above the waking city of Tasmay, focusing her attention on the glistening sea beyond. A sliver of sunny brilliance flashed just above the horizon, announcing the day's arrival. In seconds the inky sea lightened to purple, then blue; gray beaches glistened white and shadowy landscapes warmed to greens and browns.

Since arriving on Kashdune, Melinda had been aware of the strange and wonderful melodies that circulated around the island. The music that led her here was enticing and exotic—very different from the musical drama unfolding in the air as she travelled away from the island. This song didn't call to her. She had to search for the elusive harmonies she hoped would lead her to her family.

Clear your mind rang in her head as she glided through the disjointed musical waves. She was flying an erratic route as she tried to piece together a musical puzzle that eluded her. No sounds seemed to be a part of the same sequence.

The musical impulses surrounding her pounded against her skull. Try as she might, she could not untangle all the possible combinations or complete the musical jigsaw that would guide her back through the access. It wasn't the same as the melody that had brought her here— the alluring and intoxicating music of Kashdune. Even now, spinning through the jumble of sounds in the air, that wonderful melody rang clearly in her mind.

Directly below her, Joe was swimming tirelessly toward Kashdune. His focus never shifted from the music. Even the sting of recognition of something or perhaps someone important was shoved aside as he clung to the beauty of *He Aeros Musike*.

After hours of flying, still no closer to untangling the musical clues, Melinda reluctantly turned back toward the island. "You have to know the map," she conceded. "I can't connect any of the sounds to make a symphony. It just doesn't work. This must be how people have become trapped here— you have to know the key to unlock the entrance."

Comforted by the familiar melody of Kashdune, she opened her mind to the world around her. A flash of familiarity planted itself in her thoughts and she flapped toward it with all her strength.

Reaching the surf zone that circled the island, the exhausted dolphin that was Joe Whiltshire relaxed, letting the surge of the sea carry him forward. For the first time in hours he allowed his thoughts to shift away from the music, and tried to focus on his connection with Melinda. It felt strange, like she was very close. But there was nothing around him but water, and the shore was still quite a distance away. A small shadow blocked the sunshine for an instant. Joe looked to the sky at the exact instant Melinda looked down at the sea below her.

"That was incredible!" Elaine bubbled as she climbed back onto the boat.

"It must sound fantastic," Felix agreed as he helped her up the ladder.

Elaine paused. "What? Oh, yes, the music…that truly is remarkable. But I was talking about the transformations. I haven't felt so vital in ages."

Felix cringed. "You've got to be kidding, all those barnacles and blubber? Not to mention the plankton swarming through your teeth."

Elaine scowled at her son as she dried off. "I did not *have* any barnacles, and there was not one ounce of extra blubber on me, thank you very much! And as for the plankton…it's actually quite tasty."

Felix shrugged. "If you say so. What now?"

"The music is still pulling in that direction," she pointed off the bow, "toward that island. It may have something to do with Kashdune. If Melinda followed the music, she will have gone in that direction. Are Harmony and Joe upstairs?"

"Harmony is, but we haven't seen Joe since the cloud. I take it you don't know where he's gone?"

"I left him when I tried to find you in that mist. My guess would be that he's somewhere on this side of things, since he swam on ahead…let's hope so, anyway."

"I suppose we should get underway, then," Felix said as he walked toward the cabin. "The sooner we get there, the sooner we can sort all this out and get back to Dad."

"How is your father?" Elaine asked seriously.

Felix smiled. "He must be spending a lot of time thinking about the music, because I keep hearing it whenever I think about him. As soon as we find Mel and Joe and maybe even Kashdune, I'll try to let him know." He winked. "He'll be sorry he missed all the fun."

The *Nautica* cruised smoothly across the early-morning sea. "Look over there." Horace Stumpworthy pointed to a boat cruising gently over the water. "It certainly doesn't look like a fishing boat. I thought you said no one would be using the access anymore. Anyone you know?"

Fredrick Hamsong leaned forward, shaking his head. "Unfortunately, I don't have my wife's talents of perception. Sad-looking boat, isn't it? Might be someone who accidentally came through the access, although that hasn't happened in a very long time. Perhaps it's your old friends Joe Whiltshire and gang."

Stumpworthy glared, not taking his eyes off the boat. "You may be right. Too bad...if they had delayed their journey just a few hours, they might be cruising into limbo instead of heading to the island."

"Horace, that's not the purpose of altering the cloud. I don't want to see innocent people pushed into that kind of oblivion. We need only to protect Kashdune. If we're successful, no one need ever become trapped in the access; the music simply won't take them there." Fredrick watched as the other boat sailed slowly toward the island. "If that is the Huttons coming for Melinda, then at least I won't have that worry any longer."

Stumpworthy smiled and then increased the throttle. The *Nautica* sped handily across the water toward the mist.

The *Seenbetredas* chugged slowly between two buoys that marked the entrance to a harbor. Felix looked anxiously from side to side as they sailed around stone pilings and down the water pathway lined by a flotilla of fishing boats. The impression was one of a quiet Mediterranean-type scene, but as they rounded the headland a very different picture emerged. The large harbor seemed to stretch for miles, and was host to more than the usual marine vessels. The water was heaving with a floating museum of magnificent ships and boats that only a maritime historian would be able to catalogue. There were schooners and tall ships, gleaming white yachts and brightly painted Viking longships, as well as ornately carved Chinese junks.

Felix couldn't believe what he was seeing. "It's like some kind of boat show."

"Harmony, there's a dock over there," Elaine directed. "Hopefully someone can point us to the proper marina, because this surely can't be the right place."

"Oh my god!" Felix panted. "Turn around, turn around—there's a…ah…a goat…I mean a boy…wait, it's a goat-boy, and he's waving us in!"

Harmony's eyes flashed. "I have to say it is a little unusual, but let's see what we've gotten ourselves into. Why don't you two go down and say hello while I pilot this hunk in."

Elaine nodded with a glint in her eyes. "This might prove to be very interesting."

Felix wasn't so sure, and was becoming less sure the closer they got. The young man clopped across the wooden pier on his cloven hooves, directing their approach with his human hands. His face had human features, but bushy hair covered much of it, especially at the sides. He wore baggy beige shorts and a blue-checked, short-sleeved shirt, trendy-looking sunglasses, and a red baseball cap that he wore sideways.

"Welcome to Tasmay!" The boy took off his hat and bowed elegantly in greeting. Two little horns protruded from the top of his head. "My name is Meike. I'll help you tie up."

Felix and Elaine tossed him the lines, and Meike clip-clopped along the dock, securing the ropes to a metal cleat.

"That should do it," he announced. "You can shut down

the engine now," he called up to Harmony.

Harmony did, then loped down the stairs to join Elaine and Felix. The three of them didn't say a word as they stared at the unusual creature helping them.

"What brings you to Kashdune?" Meike asked.

"Kashdune! I thought you said this was Tasmay," Felix said in awe.

"The island is Kashdune; this city is Tasmay. You must be Athenite," the young man said. Felix nodded cautiously. Meike continued, "I thought so, but you never know. Every once in a while we get non-Athenite folks…their boat or plane gets into the cloud and they end up here. You seemed to know about the island, which usually means Athenite. How long are you staying?"

"So this is Kashdune…incredible," Elaine whispered. "We're not exactly sure how long we'll be here…can you direct us to a marina where we can tie up? We didn't mean to disturb your exhibition."

Meike frowned for a moment, then laughed heartily. "Oh, you mean the old boats…it's nothing special. I always forget that when people first arrive they're surprised to see all the old relics. You see, people have been arriving over the centuries and haven't returned to the other side, so their boats just stay here. You can leave your boat here, too. When you get your arrangements sorted, let me know—I'll take care of things at the marina."

Felix didn't realise that his mouth was hanging open as he stared at Meike, but Meike noticed and laughed again. "I forgot about that, too…folks from the other side aren't used to Athenites openly being Athenites. We don't get a lot of new people coming anymore, so I don't think about it much. It's weird, though—not more than a week ago this friend of Mr. Hamsong's had exactly the same reaction."

"Hamsong?" Harmony straightened noticeably.

"Yeah, Fredrick Hamsong and this bloke…ah…can't remember his name." Meike clopped over to a chair and picked up a clipboard to record the details about the boat. When he looked up, the three staring faces hadn't taken their eyes off of him. "I don't usually look like this, but I'm playing Puck in *A Midsummer Night's Dream* at my high school. There's no better way to get into character than becoming the real thing! If you're not busy tonight you should come and watch it—it's fantastic, if I do say so myself."

"Thanks," Felix mumbled, "but I don't think we'll be here very long. We're just here to pick up my sister and our friend Joe."

"Your sister?"

"Yeah, she's eleven years old, about so tall," Felix said, holding his hand to his shoulder. "Looks like a beaver," he added.

"Like a real beaver," Meike asked matter-of-factly.

"No…just a human version of one," Felix answered haltingly.

"Sorry, but she didn't come to the island this way or I'd have seen her. You might want to ask Augustina Hamsong. She always knows what's going on."

"Hamsong?" Harmony repeated.

"Fredrick's wife," Meike answered in a suspicious tone.

Harmony raised a brow. "I knew a Professor Fredrick Hamsong at university, but that was about twenty years ago…that would make him about fifty."

Meike shook his head. "Can't be the same guy—this one is only twenty-something, or maybe thirty."

Harmony smiled weakly. "Forgive me…it's just such an unusual name."

Meike shrugged. "I suppose so." He finished his paperwork and put the clipboard back on the chair. "You said you're not staying very long. Of course, that's up to you, but you shouldn't leave for a while, going through the access is dangerous if you do it too soon. You can get disoriented. The music is much more difficult to follow going that way, and one wrong turn can really mess you up. Some say people can be lost in the mist forever."

"We'll keep that in mind." Elaine climbed off the boat and walked a short distance away, and then whirled around, smiling. "This is a beautiful place. Do the Hamsongs live in town?"

"Yep. Straight up that hill, first left, then right onto the Place of the Marquis. It's a big white house with green shutters and incredible gardens."

"Thank you, Meike. We'll be back to let you know our plans as soon as we can." Elaine motioned for Felix and Harmony to join her on the dock.

"Yeah…ah…thanks," added Felix as he jumped down, trying not to stare at the horns.

CHAPTER TWENTY-TWO

Joe knew that there was only one way to find out if the bird that had flown over him was indeed Melinda, and that was a complicated transformation of changing directly from dolphin to bird—without getting his feathers wet. It took split-second timing and the reflexes of someone who was in good shape. Joe was already exhausted from his journey—and as for his general physical condition, he wasn't as fit as he used to be.

In a normal transformation, he would freeze his movements and concentrate on change. In this transformation, an entire sequence of activity had to be accomplished with simultaneous execution. He had to swim with enough speed to leave the water, transforming immediately as he did and, without time to adjust to his new body, fly swiftly against gravity that would draw him back toward the waves. It was a lot like an old-fashioned magic trick, where an object thrown into the air instantly becomes a pigeon and flutters away. Only this wasn't magic—it was real, and there was no room for mistakes. Failure might even kill him.

Time was not on his side. Somewhere in the sky, he knew Melinda was thinking about the same sequence in reverse. He couldn't shake the image of her transforming into something only vaguely resembling a dolphin, then plummeting into the sea from nearly a kilometer above the sea.

Please, Melinda, he thought. *I'll come to you…don't do anything!*

"Well, I'm not getting any drier," he sighed as he dove under the water. He leveled off about six meters below the surface; then, thrusting his powerful tail, he rocketed up, cutting through the water like a missile being launched into the sky. He flew high above the surface of the water for several seconds, arching his body naturally on descent, but failed to even attempt the transformation. He splashed back into the sea and tried again, then again, and again. There simply wasn't enough time for him to manoeuvre.

It's no use…I've got to try to communicate with her some other way and tell her to meet me on land, he thought as he scanned the heavens. But as he spun around, he couldn't even see a speck in the blue cloudless sky anymore. *Maybe it wasn't her*, he tried to convince himself, *or maybe she simply didn't see me.*

It was no use. He knew it had been Melinda—he had felt her presence with intensity, unlike anything he had ever experienced before. She wasn't in the sky, but he could feel she was still very close by. That meant only one thing: she had to be in the water.

His exhaustion evaporated as adrenaline rushed through his system and he plunged under the water. His sense of her presence was acute, and he knew he was fighting limited time to get to her. If she were injured, she wouldn't survive for long.

Pumping his tail, he sped off in the direction of the signal his brain was receiving. He could feel the vibration of a life force coming closer. If it *was* Melinda, then she was alive! He darted through the water, drawing closer and closer to the source of the signal. Only it wasn't Melinda. Swimming torpedo-fashion toward him was an open-mouthed shark of gigantic proportions. Staring at those gaping teeth, Joe wondered if his luck had at last truly run out.

"Large, white, and green shutters...this must be the place."
Harmony huffed. "I definitely need to get back into
shape—that was one big hill!"

She, Elaine, and Felix walked along the gravel pathway
through the front garden of the beautiful estate. When at
last they reached the entrance, they paused, each wearing
a nearly identical expression of uncertainty. "Let's hope
we're at the right place," Harmony whispered.

"What if there's n-nothing home?" Felix grimaced,
staring unblinkingly at the door.

Harmony smirked. "You mean *no one*, don't you?"

Felix looked at her wide-eyed. "I guess so. But even
if someth...some*one* is here, what if they don't know
anything?" His voice shook even though he was trying to
play it cool and calm.

"Then I don't know what we'll do. But we have to start
somewhere." Elaine shuddered. "I do wish Joe was here...
he could tell us something."

Seconds pounded away, but it felt like they'd been
standing frozen for hours. Then in one single movement,
they all clenched their fists and reached up to knock. But
they didn't have a chance before the door was swung
open on its own. A tall, dark-haired woman greeted them
pleasantly. Her shrewd expression gave the impression that
she had been expecting their arrival.

"Hello. You must be Elaine...Felix...and Harmony, if
I'm not mistaken." Augustina grinned at the three fists
raised to the door, now only centimeters from her nose.
"I've been eager for your arrival. My name is Augustina;
please come inside." She held the door open and gestured
for them to enter.

Elaine and Harmony slowly lowered their arms and
followed Augustina as she guided them into the foyer.

Felix remained a moment in bemused suspension, his eyes wide and his mouth hanging ajar. At last he realized his hand was still raised and the others were already inside. He trotted after them to join the strange and silent procession marching through the house.

His heart was pounding like a timpani against his ribs, excitement racing through him and replacing his fear. This woman knew about their arrival long before they came to her house. That wasn't too hard to explain—the boy at the marina must have informed her. But that couldn't account for the fact that she knew their names. That had to mean that Augustina knew Melinda!

Augustina swung around and looked calmly into his eyes. "I do know your sister. I was hoping that she would be with you. I'm afraid she has mastered the ability to mask her thoughts…of course, that's a talent to be proud of." She smiled then turned her gaze upon Elaine. "But a nuisance for parents…don't you agree?"

"So you've seen her," Elaine breathed. "Oh, thank goodness. Is she all right?"

Augustina didn't reply at once, turning away and sweeping through the house once more, finally stopping on the terrace in the rear garden. When everyone had gathered in the brilliant sunshine, she spoke again.

"She left early this morning to find you." Augustina's posture was relaxed as she motioned for her guests to sit around the patio table. "Please let me offer you refreshments. How long do you expect to stay? We have guest quarters that you will find quite comfortable."

Elaine wasn't at all interested in refreshments or guest quarters. "You said that Melinda left to find us, but we haven't seen her. Where could she have gone?"

"As I said, she has hidden her thoughts. I can only tell you what I hope happened. Of course, if she has found Joe, they may attempt a journey through the access—especially if they think you may still be on the other side." Augustina was speaking very matter-of-factly, as if she were talking about an adult rather than an eleven-year-old girl.

"You know Joe?" Felix asked incredulously.

"I've never met him, but I know him and all of you through Melinda's thoughts. As you know, it would be dangerous for Joe to make the journey again so soon after his arrival…I believe Meike may have told you about the hazard."

"Meike! The boy at the marina! So he did call you," Felix sighed.

Augustina looked confused for an instant. "Call me? I'm not sure I understand…what would he call me?" Then, shaking her head, she exclaimed, "Of course, you mean telephoned—no, no, we don't have telephones on the island. We have other ways of communicating here." Elaine shifted, obviously impatient, and Augustina looked at her kindly. "I know Melinda will be fine, whatever the outcome."

Elaine's eyes flashed dangerously. "You seem to know a lot of things," she seethed. "She's only eleven years old, out there by herself. How can you be so certain she's safe?"

Augustina squinted. "She is an Athenite, and has a very insightful mind." She saw the discomfort on the faces of her guests and laughed heartily. "You really don't know very much about Kashdune, do you? This island is our last bastion. The majority of the people here are Athenites." Augustina stood up and walked to the edge of the terrace. "The history of our people," she said, "can be found here."

"Are you one, too…an Athenite?" Felix's voice broke over the question.

"Of course." Augustina looked at them all as if they were small children. "Athenites have many talents besides the ability to transform. Another of our talents is extrasensory perception. When we know someone, we can develop our ability to connect with them telepathically." She turned her gaze to Felix. "I know about Melinda's special connection with—"

"Joe!" Felix shrieked.

"That's right. But after all, those are very special relationships. The type of telepathy I am talking about is more common. All Athenites have the ability to know other people's thoughts and feelings. Since meeting Melinda, I have grown to know her, as well as the important people in her life. I was able to connect with you through her. But when Melinda masked her thoughts, I lost touch with her—and with all of you.

"The connection she has with Joe is much stronger and cannot be broken. No matter what happens, Melinda will be able to sense Joe's well-being, as he will hers." She looked directly at Felix.

Harmony closed her eyes. What they were being told was extraordinary: mental telepathy, an entire civilization of Athenites living on an obscure island in what appeared to be another dimension…was it real? Could they trust what Augustina was telling them? And who was she, anyway?

Harmony tried to bring a picture of Augustina forward in her mind, and shivers scurried all over her body as she realized that she couldn't pull up the features of the woman sitting right across from her. Her eyes sprang open to find Augustina staring at her.

"There is a lot for you all to learn about our people and Kashdune," Augustina said, smiling.

For Felix, everything was moving too fast, and yet nothing seemed to be happening at all. "Maybe we can talk about all that stuff later…right now, isn't there anything you can do to help us?" Felix pleaded.

Augustina raised an eyebrow. "I'm afraid I can't. Melinda's destiny is in her own hands now."

CHAPTER TWENTY-THREE

Deadly fear didn't give Joe any more energy. He wanted to transform into something to dissuade the shark, but to do so meant using strength and concentration that he simply didn't have.

The creature's huge jaws were open, as if grinning at the poor, helpless sap that was about to satisfy its hunger pangs. As it drew closer, so did the feeling that Melinda was nearby. Alarm struck Joe's mind like a bolt of lightning. It was obvious—the shark had already eaten her, and it had swallowed her whole! It was definitely big enough to do it. But she *was* still alive—he could feel it. The problem was, how could he get to her without suffering the same fate? An image of Melinda sitting inside the shark's belly, like the old fable of Jonah and the Whale, flashed in his mind.

Staring at the rows of incredibly large, incredibly sharp teeth made him realize how impossible killing the predator would be. Plus, even if he successfully destroyed the shark, Melinda would almost definitely die before he could pull her to safety. There was only one course to save her—to save them both. He had to lure the beast to land and then kill it. He would have to use himself as bait.

The desire to save his young friend brought out the reserves of energy his body desperately required, and he

darted toward the island. His plan was working so far—
the shark stayed close behind, right on his tail. Joe surged
forward, swimming a zigzagging course to avoid those
wretched teeth. The shark swam after him, always staying
close but not close enough to strike. Joe had to keep it that
way—he didn't want the beast to get discouraged and turn
away, but he didn't want it to taste success, either.

Joe surfaced to take in a breath, glimpsing the sandy
beaches of the island coming rapidly closer. The shark
followed him, staying just below the water with only its
enormous fin cutting the surface. Once again Joe looked
at the colossal fish behind him. Its evil smiling expression
gave the impression that it was enjoying this game of
follow the leader.

At last Joe could feel the surf pulling and propelling him
toward the land. If he could kill the shark now, he might be
able to push the carcass to shore and free Melinda. It was
a huge gamble, but it seemed like his only option. He leapt
free of the water, arching his body so that when he dove
back in he would be facing the shark. Now face to face with
his attacker—its huge, grinning face seemed to be laughing
at him—Joe lunged, trying to smash the nose of the beast.
The shark veered away. Joe attacked from another angle.
The shark simply swam away from the impending blow.
It was a mad scene, like a bullfight, except in this case the
shark was the matador, with the bull played by the dolphin
version of Joe Whiltshire. Over and over Joe attempted to
bash the shark, and each time he failed to do so.

Finally, after several minutes of this bizarre exchange,
the shark began to swim away. Joe was exhausted and felt
a surge of victory, but that only lasted seconds. Melinda
was still inside.

Joe was completely drained of energy, yet he swam
on, trying in vain to catch up. The pursuit didn't last
long, because the water was now very shallow. The shark
stopped, swaying its mammoth tail, then twisted its body

around. As the gargantuan animal came about, Joe noticed a rather remarkable quality to its smiling expression.

"Melinda," he whistled, "you sly shark! I should have known. Sharks don't usually have freckles and big blue eyes."

Augustina adjusted her gaze, looking out over the heads of her guests. "I hope some of your questions will be answered very shortly. If you'll excuse me." She glided around the table and back through the open door into the dining room.

As soon as she had gone, Felix leaned back in his chair. "What are we going to do now?"

"Let's get out of here," Harmony grouched as she stood up. "That woman can read our thoughts, and she hasn't told us how we can find Melinda. We should split up and search the island. Joe must be here by now. If we find him, he may be able to lead us to her."

Felix slid his chair back in preparation for their departure, but Elaine stayed where she was. "Let's wait to see how Augustina plans to answer our questions," she said, surprisingly calm now. "If nothing else, she should be able to tell us something about this island."

Harmony nodded resignedly and sat back down. Felix, a disagreeable scowl etched on his face, did the same. He rested his elbows on the table, turning his head to look inside the house. "There's someone else here!" he whispered.

"Who?" Harmony and Elaine asked in unison.

"How should I know?" he hissed. "I don't know anyone who lives on Kashdune. The only thing I saw was that she was talking to a man."

"Joe?" Elaine eagerly leaned forward, trying to see inside the house.

"I couldn't tell who he was. You'd think that if it was Joe he'd come out here. Unless…" Felix raised an eyebrow.

"Unless what?" Harmony tilted her head anxiously.

Felix looked from Harmony to his mother. "Unless she doesn't really want us to see him…or…"

Elaine gasped. "Melinda?" Felix nodded.

Augustina reappeared on the terrace almost before Felix could close his mouth. "Are you sure I can't get you something to drink or eat?" Everyone shook their heads as they waited for some kind of explanation. "No, I'm sorry, that wasn't Joe," she answered, although no one had asked the question aloud. "Please believe me—if I knew exactly where your friend Joe or Melinda could be found, I would tell you immediately. The man I was talking with is Albert Easton, a colleague of my husband's, who was simply dropping off some data about one of their projects."

Felix's face reddened and Elaine frowned at Augustina's apparent eavesdropping into their thoughts. The woman bowed her head.

"Please forgive me. I'll try not to use my telepathy so freely…I'm sure it can be a little daunting when you're not used to it." She smiled and walked around the table. "You may find this interesting, though. Albert is human—one of the few who live on the island. His plane was caught in the access in a freak accident many years ago. It is very rare, especially these days, but every once in a great while a human stumbles into Kashdune."

"What do we have here?" A man's voice boomed from the other side of the garden, startling everyone—including Augustina, who, up until then, seemed to know everything.

Augustina melted into a warm smile. "Fredrick, you startled me! You're getting exceptionally good at masking yourself…I had no idea you were home." She laughed. "Please come and say hello to our guests—Melinda's mother, Elaine, her brother Felix, and Harmony Melpot. They have just arrived." She twisted back to face the table. "I'd like to introduce you to my husband, Fredrick Hamsong."

Fredrick eagerly crossed the terrace. "This is indeed a pleasure. Splendid, you all made it through the access. I was worried that we were cutting it a bit close."

"Cutting what a bit close?" Felix snarled, but his voice was drowned out by Harmony, who had jumped to her feet, nearly knocking over her chair.

"Fredrick Hamsong!" she shrieked.

"Harmony Melpot," he rejoined with very little surprise in his voice. "How long has it been? At least ten or fifteen years, hasn't it?"

"More like twenty!" Harmony walked haltingly over to shake his hand. As she got closer, she gasped. "You don't look a day older than you did when you taught at my university."

Fredrick Hamsong smiled. "It's a very long story—centuries old, in fact. One that I will be only too happy to share with you. But before we get into anything like that, there's something I need to tell you, and I think you had better sit down."

"Has something happened to Melinda?" Elaine cried, jumping to her feet in alarm.

Fredrick motioned for her to take her seat. "No, nothing about Melinda." Elaine and Harmony slowly sat down as Hamsong began. "We all have ghosts from our past, people that we might wish never to see again, but that have a habit of surprising us…"

Hamsong hadn't completed his speech when another man spoke up from inside the dining room. "Hello, Elaine, Felix…Harmony." A figure stepped out into the sunshine and bowed graciously to them all.

Elaine and Harmony instinctively jerked round to confirm that Felix was still himself. Then all three stared in horrified confusion at the man who appeared to be the spitting image of Horace Stumpworthy.

"Surprised to see me?" Stumpworthy smiled slyly as he sauntered toward the table. "Thanks to Fredrick, I have completely recovered from the wolfbane poisoning and now have a new life here on Kashdune."

Elaine's eyes narrowed at the man who, less than a year ago, had tried to destroy her family. "I don't know what's going on here, but I assure you: if you have harmed my daughter, you will pay dearly," she hissed.

Fredrick stepped closer and looked kindly down at Elaine. "Horace has done nothing. None of us would think of harming Melinda. I hope she will be along any time, but for now I suggest you all take the opportunity to freshen up and relax a bit while Horace and I conclude some work. With any luck Melinda might be here by then, and I can tell you everything you want to know. Now, if you'll excuse me." He stepped around the table, nodding to Stumpworthy, who followed him inside.

The hair on the back of Felix's neck was bristling. He felt trapped, in this place where people were obviously quite chummy with a man he regarded as an enemy. Felix couldn't let them simply walk away without at least some answers.

"Mr. Hamsong, what if Joe and Melinda go back through the access?" he called after them.

Fredrick turned to face him. "I would expect that your friend Joe would be much too tired to want to try." He turned to go inside the house and whispered, "At least I hope so."

CHAPTER TWENTY-FOUR

A splash in the breakers brought Evan to his feet. And it was a good thing it did, because he had lost track of time and he had no idea how long he'd been sitting on that rock. He looked out at the rolling surf, hoping to see a dolphin or a flying fish, but nothing danced above the waves. At last he saw what had made the splash, though at first they were hard to identify, with only their small heads poking out of the frothing waves. Two giant sea turtles were surfing up onto the shore, their strong flippers digging trenches into the sand.

Evan had taken the beach path home from school, the route he usually took when he had a lot on his mind. Today his head pounded with only one pestering thought: Melinda. She had left that morning without a word to anyone—no "thanks for having me," no "see you later," not even a casual wave as she flew away. He had looked forward to bringing her to school with him. She obviously hadn't felt the same. So he'd spent his entire day brooding.

The turtles were a lovely distraction. He would have watched them for a long time if they hadn't sprouted feathers. Evan sighed. "They're only Athenites." He turned to leave, but a weird movement caught his eye and he jerked back around for a closer look. Something was definitely peculiar about these turtles, and just a tiny bit familiar. While one of them smoothly changed into a falcon, the other one struggled, maintaining its hard shell and sporting something resembling a rabbit's tail.

"Melinda?" Evan whispered as he crept across the sand for a closer look. The bird-turtle-rabbit-shaped creature jerked its beaked head toward him. "It is you!" he gasped when he looked into her eyes. "What's wrong with you? You know how to become a bird."

Melinda tried to shrug, but her shell prevented the movement. "I don't know what's wrong. I was a bird when I found Joe, then I turned into a shark so we could swim together. Actually, I tried to change into a dolphin, but that didn't quite work. Then we both transformed into turtles so that we could come onto shore." She wore a perplexed expression. "Except for the shark thing, I didn't have any problems."

"Maybe you're just tired," Evan suggested.

Melinda eyed him suspiciously. "How did you know what I said?"

Evan smiled. "Because you were just talking to me," he shot back.

"Do you speak turtle?" Melinda didn't give him a chance to answer, glancing at Joe who was eyeing Evan apprehensively. "This is Joe," she said to Evan. "I've got to figure out a way to talk with him, like using my telewhatsit."

Evan winced. "Telepathy?"

"Yeah. Telepathy."

"Why don't you just talk to him? You don't need to read minds when you're standing right next to someone."

"And how am I supposed to do that?" She grimaced as she looked down at herself. "We're not exactly the same species anymore, are we?"

Evan shook his head. "Don't tell me—Athenites from the other side can't communicate with different species? You have a lot to learn."

Melinda sighed. "Maybe so, but that won't help me right now. I need to change so Joe and I can go back to the access. My mom, Felix, and Harmony were travelling with him, but they got separated. We need to find them."

Evan shook his head. "If he just went through the access to get here, then he can't go back through again for a while. It has something to do with the impact the cloud has on your brain. My parents can explain. Besides, if *he's* here, then the others might be too."

Melinda dropped her head. "I hope you're right."

Suddenly Evan remembered the anger that had ruined his day, and he folded his arms in disgust. "You know, it's not good manners to just leave without a word."

Melinda looked sheepish. "I'm sorry about that. I really missed my family and wanted to be with them. I was afraid I might be stuck here forever without them."

"It's not such a bad place to be *stuck*, as you put it."

"I know, but you'd feel the same if you were without your parents."

Evan narrowed his eyes. "I still wouldn't have been so rude!"

Melinda pursed her lips but couldn't think of anything to say.

Without waiting for her response, Evan turned and began squawking at Joe. When he turned back to Melinda, he looked like he was in a better mood. "Joe thinks you had better change properly so that you don't attract attention." He laughed.

"He's never been in a place like this where Athenites are free to change as they please," Melinda explained.

Evan pointed at her, giggling uncontrollably. "He still has a point. I don't think I've ever seen anything that looked like that, not even on Kashdune."

Joe couldn't get comfortable in the clothes Evan had loaned him. The trousers were at least two inches too short and uncomfortably tight around his waist, while the shirt was straining at the buttons, leaving gaps between each one.

"Well, if it isn't Joe Whiltshire, fashion guru!" Harmony chortled as Joe joined the others in the Hamsongs' garden. "I can see why you didn't want to dress in your own clothes—this ensemble is much more becoming."

"I don't know if anyone will go for it, Joe," Elaine joined in. "Not everyone can carry off that look, but then, I've never been an expert in fashion trends."

"Aren't you two the comedians…maybe you should shelve your old careers and go on the stage," Joe sneered back. He pulled at the trousers, trying and failing to lengthen the legs. Melinda giggled and Felix blushed at Joe's undignified appearance. Joe frowned. "I'll get down to the boat after dinner, if that's all right with you lot. For now, you'll just have to put up with it."

Elaine smiled as she looked from Joe to Melinda. "I can hardly believe that we're all together on Kashdune," she sighed. "I only wish Jake were here, too."

"At least we know he's okay," Felix added.

Harmony nodded. "That must be quite a mind connection you two have," she said to Felix, before turning to Joe. "What I don't understand is, since you share the same type of connection with Melinda, why did it take *you* so long to figure out that Melinda was the shark?"

Joe looked guilty. "It's such a new feeling. I'll admit that I don't know how to read it properly. When we were out there," he nodded in the direction of the sea, "I could sense her, but…"

Melinda giggled. "You thought that the shark had swallowed me…WHOLE!"

Joe looked uncomfortably around at the others. "Can we please talk about anything besides me?"

At that moment, Augustina glided out to the terrace. She set a tray of cutlery and plates on the garden table and then glanced at Joe. "I see you're not exactly the same size as Fredrick," she said, trying to stifle a laugh. "If you're uncomfortable you can always change into something else."

"I'm fine for now," Joe announced with as much dignity as he could manage. "As I was just saying, I'll gather my clothes from the boat after dinner."

Augustina straightened, a puzzled look on her face. "I didn't mean change into other clothes. I was talking about changing into something like fur, or even feathers— however you might feel most comfortable."

Joe looked at her as if she'd just arrived from Mars. "Ah…I'll be fine for now," he replied slowly.

Augustina bowed her head, turned, and went back inside the house.

Joe sighed. "I don't know if I can get used to a totally Athenite society. Living openly like they do here is really wild. I suppose it just takes some getting used to."

Felix nodded. "I know what you mean. It is totally weird—half-animal, half-human creatures on every corner. But you should watch what you think around her." He nodded his head after Augustina.

"Why?" Joe asked.

"Augustina reads minds," Melinda added, her feet flailing as she attempted a handstand on the grass. "But she doesn't do it all the time. All Athenites are supposed to be able to do it."

"You're joking, right?" Joe looked at Elaine and Harmony, who shook their heads.

Melinda, having failed at another handstand, crumpled onto the grass. "Did you know that she can disappear too?"

"What are you talking about? No one can disappear," Felix piped up.

Elaine shook her head. "I don't think she means *vanish*…"

"Yes I do," Melinda answered calmly. "I've seen her myself. Well, what I mean is…I couldn't see her, and then I could. I'll bet if you think about her right now, you won't be able to remember what she looks like. It's all connected." She got to her feet and attempted another handstand.

Joe rubbed his face. "Like I said, this is all going to take some getting used to."

Warm air and clear skies, an abundance of night-blooming fragrant flowers, and the twilight song of strange and beautifully colored birds enhanced the tone of the evening. It was all so lovely that Felix wondered if Augustina had the power to control the environment as well. As she cleared the table after their two-hour feast, Augustina leaned forward and whispered in his ear, "No, I don't influence nature. I think it's perfect the way it is." Felix shivered at the intrusion and smiled at her weakly.

Fredrick Hamsong cleared his throat and tapped his glass to get everyone's attention. "Welcome to our home," he said, raising his glass to his guests. "You have found each other, and we have found new friends…here's to Kashdune and *He Aeros Musike*, the magic that brought us together!"

"Hear, hear!" everyone called.

Fredrick drank to the toast and then set his glass carefully down. "I'm sorry that Jake could not be with us tonight, but as we have learned from Felix, he has returned to good health. To Jake!"

"To Jake," everyone cheered.

"I am only sorry that Horace was unable to join us tonight," Fredrick continued.

"Not me!" Harmony, Joe, and Elaine all cried.

Fredrick gave a faltering smile and bowed his head. "I

know all about your past difficulties, but it is always best to look forward and let bygones be bygones." He took another sip of his drink, letting silence fall around the table. "Now—I have promised you all a story. You may find it a strange tale, but you must remember that truth is often stranger than fiction.

"I was born a very long time ago," he began. "It was a time of innocence, before superstitious thinking invaded the world. I lived in the era of freedom for Athenites, when humans accepted us and we lived together as one people. It is the history that is recorded in mythology or told as fairy tales, passed down through generations as nothing but charming fables. But everything I will tell you is absolutely true.

"When I was a young man, I began following birds on their migrations to see where they were drawn to and why. I discovered that they followed their own music, navigating thousands of miles to the same places year after year. I then began tracking the melodies that attracted other animals. It was fascinating to see how they navigated, following the sounds that were essential to their survival.

"One year, while flying with a flock of swallows, I travelled to the edge of Western Europe. It was there that I first heard the music of Kashdune. It had a pull like nothing I'd ever experienced, and I followed as if without choice. As you all know from your own experience, it is a difficult thing to resist.

"I was a very long way from home, but I never thought about turning back—the pull of that music was too powerful. So, all by myself, in a world completely uncharted and unknown by the civilizations at the time, I journeyed, never stopping, until the music released me and I landed on Kashdune.

"There were, not too surprisingly, other Athenites living on the island. It seemed I wasn't the only one to fall victim to the siren song that pulls people here. Nor was I to be the last. From here I would witness the changes to the island and the world for generations to come.

"I had transformed into a bird, in preparation to leave the island, when I flew over a remarkably clear river. The sight of that crystal-clear water beckoned, and I couldn't resist taking a drink. Within seconds I involuntarily transformed back into a human body. It was the strangest transformation I'd ever experienced—and my last, I'm sad to say. The water proved to be life sustaining, but with the good comes the bad. For the gift of eternal life, we forfeit our ability to transform."

Felix slammed his glass down, having realized a little too late that his glass was filled with water.

Augustina smiled warmly. "There's no need to worry. We have other water supplies on the island that are completely safe to drink."

Harmony stared at Fredrick in awe. "Your story is incredible, and it explains a lot about you. You were the youngest professor I ever had at university. You can imagine how odd it was seeing again after all these years when you haven't aged a day."

Fredrick nodded. "For that very reason, it has always been difficult for me to keep in touch with people on the other side. People are expected to age and, as you see, I do not."

Joe stared at the water in his glass, smiling absently at his reflection. "The infamous Fountain of Youth. Too bad Ponce de Lyon didn't listen for the music."

Fredrick laughed. "Poor fellow. I actually met him once, but in Florida, where he was convinced he would find the magical elixir. I felt rather sorry for him, mainly because he was right about its existence. Most people, however, thought he was mad. Of course, I couldn't tell him where to find the water; it would have jeopardised Kashdune's Athenite population. At that time in history, humans had long forgotten all they ever knew about the existence of

Athenites. Fear and superstition made it dangerous for us to exist openly.

"Eternal Water is rarely used anymore, only in cases of severe infection or other life-threatening disorders, and only with the consent of a well-informed adult. Eternal life is not always a gift." Fredrick sighed. "Especially when you lose the gifts of being Athenite."

"I'm never going to drink that water," Melinda vowed, shaking her head.

Fredrick laughed softly. "Let's hope that you will never need to. For me it was an accident; for others, taking the water is a necessity. It has been known to cure many diseases—or in Horace's case, uncomfortable conditions."

"That's why he's not a lemming," Harmony sighed.

Fredrick nodded. "I shared what little I had with me when I found him on the other side, and he's made a startling recovery. But as with so many things, there are consequences. I won't deny that it's a shock for an Athenite to lose their abilities. I miss flight the most, even after all these years. And I never had the opportunity to develop other skills, like Augustina has done. Still, I have many animal senses and telepathic powers; I can hear the sounds of *He Aeros Musike*; I have a beautiful family here on Kashdune. I consider myself very lucky. While Horace misses his talents now, he is an intelligent man and will learn to be fulfilled in his new life."

Fredrick looked around the table at the questioning looks on his guests' faces.

"I welcome your questions. We have nothing to hide on Kashdune. It's on the other side that you must mask who and what you really are. But before we go on, I need to tell you…ahem…" He coughed. " Ahem…I need…ahem…"

"Fredrick, are you all right?" Harmony pushed back from the table and trotted to his side.

"Ahem…I have something…ahem…im-por…" He could no longer speak as his body was racked with violent spasms.

"Fredrick, are you choking on something?" Harmony demanded. He didn't speak but shook his head. "Does he have any allergies that might have triggered this?" she asked Augustina frantically.

"No—none. This has never happened before," Augustina cried.

"He seems to be having a reaction to something." Harmony grabbed his wrist and took his pulse. "Maybe we could use that water he was talking about—do you have any?"

Augustina nodded, jumped to her feet, and darted inside the house. She returned carrying a small carafe containing the clear liquid. Before they could administer even one drop, Hamsong's spasms stopped, his pallor drained to a pasty white, and he collapsed forward onto the table.

Harmony did a quick examination, frustrated and confused. "I haven't practiced medicine in years. All I can tell you right now is that he's alive and fighting to stay that way. We need to get him to a bed—quickly. I wish Jake was here!"

After everyone else rushed inside with Fredrick, Felix and Melinda were left alone on the terrace. "That was horrible," Felix said, a shiver running down his back.

Melinda nodded. "Maybe it was just something he ate."

"I hope he'll be okay. If that water is as powerful as he said, he'll probably recover." Felix walked across the terrace, staring out at the moonlit garden. "You know when Harmony said she wished Dad was here?" Melinda nodded. "Well, I got this really weird feeling. I know he's okay now, but something else is going on with him, only I don't know what it is."

Melinda walked across the grass to a large shrub of violet flowers. "I know the feeling. I sense strange things all the time that are connected to what Joe is experiencing. Most of the time I can't figure them out, but I'm getting better at it."

Felix looked up at the dark sky. He was startled by how few stars there were. "This place is bizarre. It's like we're on a different world. I can't understand how all these things are possible."

"That's not surprising. You had a hard time even accepting that we're Athenites."

"I know, but some of this stuff should be impossible— like disappearing, and living for thousands of years. Do you believe that Fredrick has really lived so long?"

Melinda shrugged. "Yeah, I guess so."

"I wonder what he was trying to tell us. It sounded like he wanted us to know something important. It's a bit strange that he started having fits right when he was about to tell us."

Melinda nodded. "I was thinking the same thing."

"I wish I could read minds," Felix said tentatively.

Melinda gave a thoughtful smile. "Maybe you're closer to doing that than you think."

CHAPTER TWENTY-FIVE

After leaving the hospital, Jake had returned to the hotel, where he followed the doctor's prescription for rest and relaxation. He spent all his waking hours reclining in a comfortable chair on the balcony. The first two days passed uneventfully. On the third day however, and every day since, bizarre thoughts and visions had invaded his mind. He wondered if he might be on the path to madness.

At first he reckoned that he might simply be experiencing some kind of strange déjà vu. He thought he must have been recalling childhood fantasies of horned goat-boys and whiskered cat-girls. Maybe it was just the nightmares he'd suffered as a child resurfacing. But when he searched his mind, he could not recall any such phantoms ever invading his sleep.

"I'm getting delusional and suffering some temporary hallucinations. It happens when a body goes through shock," he tried to calm himself. But no matter how he tried to explain away his condition, he still worried.

Many of these apparitions included Harmony, Joe, Elaine, and Melinda. Other people, whom he did not know, would also flash into his mind from time to time. Most alarmingly, Horace Stumpworthy made an appearance or two. Stranger still was that these pictures were always accompanied by the shadow of an emotion that Jake couldn't understand. He felt happiness when he was worried, excitement when he was bored.

Felix had never appeared in these images, which he thought especially strange, since Felix had been very much on his mind. "That's it," he announced one day to an annoying fly circling his head. "I'm seeing the world through Felix's eyes!"

To test his theory, Jake decided to complete this telepathic circuit. In deep meditative thought, Jake concentrated on his recovery, sending out signals to his son that his health was improving daily. He told Felix, through his thoughts, that soon they would all be reunited and not to worry about a thing. It didn't take long before a feeling of total relief washed over him. "He knows! He knows I'm okay," Jake called out, frightening away a small bird that had been resting on the railing.

The days passed much more quickly after that, as Jake worked to decipher the language of his telepathic connection with his son. Through Felix, he knew all was well with his family and friends; he learned about Kashdune, met the Hamsongs, and cringed at the disturbing reappearance of Horace Stumpworthy.

One day Jake woke up feeling the best he had since suffering his injuries. It was very early, before most people at the hotel would even consider tackling the day. He walked out onto the balcony, where he was greeted by welcoming bands of golden light, announcing that the sun would soon make its dramatic appearance in the deep violet sky. Down on the beach, a group of shorebirds, taking advantage of the hours before humans would invade their hunting ground, darted across the sand in search of breakfast. They were beautiful, with their long, stick-like legs and elegant, slender bodies, dancing as the surf lapped the shore. He watched, mesmerized by the ballet of these creatures in tune with the rhythmic pulse of the sea and…

"The music!" he screeched. "They're dancing to the sound of the music in the air and I can hear it!" And indeed he could. The vibrant music floated on the breeze; its intoxicating melody encouraged him to follow. He didn't resist. Within seconds he was airborne captivated by the music of Kashdune.

"I'm afraid there's been no change," Harmony announced when she walked out into the garden the morning after Fredrick's collapse. "He seems to have slipped into a coma." She sat down at the table. Elaine and Joe were drinking their coffee and Felix and Melinda had just finished their breakfast. Harmony glanced at the house, then looked around the table. "He's aging, too. He looks at least ten years older than he did last night," she whispered. "It would appear that his body is catching up with his age, and the water isn't helping. Maybe it's not the gift of eternal life after all."

Melinda's face screwed up. "But he's *really* old! Shouldn't he just turn to dust or something?"

"Melinda!" Felix hissed, though he was wondering the same thing himself. He turned to Harmony and asked, "Shouldn't they call a doctor?"

"There was a doctor here very early this morning, but she said there was nothing she could do, especially since the water isn't helping. I really don't know what's going to happen to him. Before last night, I'd never heard of anyone living as long as he says he has." Harmony pushed back from the table and stood up. "All I can suggest is to prepare ourselves for the worst."

Felix shrieked—but it wasn't Harmony's news that had caused his wide-eyed, open-mouthed hysteria. Elaine turned to see what had upset him; then, she too, gasped. Harmony's almost deafening screech rocked the table, and even Joe let out the tiniest whimper at this very bizarre spectacle.

It was, by far, the strangest thing they had observed on the island. Floating out of the house was Augustina's peacock-blue dress, and supporting the garment was what appeared to be a watery form in the shape of Augustina. It was like looking through a glass statue filled with opaque, gelatinous liquid. As she glided passed, they could see cloudy images of the garden through her body as if they were looking through the thick glass of an old-fashioned cola bottle.

The only one in the group not fazed by the scene was Melinda. As her family and friends gaped, she got up from the table and ran over to her. "Augustina! It's going to be all right—I know it is."

Augustina's glass-like head turned toward Melinda. "You have many gifts. Let's hope you have the talent to predict a happy ending." She wrapped her transparent arms around Melinda as the others watched in amazement. "No matter what happens, we are prepared," she said. "Nothing in life is ever guaranteed, even the eternal life given by the water. We must be brave and see how destiny will treat us."

She looked up, noticing for the first time the wide-eyed stares that were focused on her.

"Please forgive me. I have faded and have obviously surprised you. I transformed so that I could be with you without showing the sadness on my face, as I knew that would worry you. I had thought by not vanishing completely you might be able to accept this form of transformation with greater ease. I see I was wrong. Would you prefer that I change?"

Joe looked at the watery aberration that was talking to them as if this were the most normal thing in the world. *Man oh man! Like I said, this place will take getting used to*, he thought, then, realizing that she could read his mind, wished he hadn't.

"Ah, no…no, we're, ahem…fine…yes…we're fine with your… ah…yes, yes, we're fine."

"Well said," Felix mumbled. He looked with awe at Augustina. *Now that is something I wish I could do*, he thought.

Augustina's crystal-like eyes sparkled at him. "I would be happy to teach you this skill." Felix blushed, nodding shyly.

With her arm still wrapped around Melinda's shoulder, Augustina looked around the table. "Evan refuses to leave his father's side, which I understand. I have sent word to Fredrick's business associate, Albert Easton, and to Horace to alert them to his condition. They are both very concerned. Albert will be along later, but Horace will be here very soon. He said he must speak to all of you at once."

"What does he want with us?" barked Felix.

Augustina smiled weakly. "I'm sorry, but I can't tell you, simply because I don't know. Horace has a mind that is difficult to understand. It's like a textbook, full of figures and facts. His thoughts are always filled with these things, so I have no way of telling what he is feeling or thinking. I'm afraid we will all have to wait to see what he has to say."

"Augustina!" Horace Stumpworthy called as he entered the house. Augustina noticeably jumped.

"He is an amazing man," she said, shaking her see-through head. "I can't even tell when he is nearby."

Stumpworthy hurried out onto the terrace, kissing Augustina's glassy cheeks and hugging her fondly. "I can't believe this is happening. I came as quickly as I could."

"Thank you, Horace. You are a good friend. Would you like to see him?"

"Of course, but I must talk to you all before I do. Did Fredrick tell you about the access?" He met each person's eyes as he looked around the table.

"What about the access?" Joe snorted.

Felix looked up at Stumpworthy. "He was trying to tell us something right before he collapsed. Maybe it was about the access."

"I've no doubt," Stumpworthy said with a frown. "It's very important that you know what is taking place. I know this is a terrible time to tell you considering Fredrick's condition…"

"No, go on—what's more important than Fredrick's life?" Harmony sneered.

"Not more important, my dear friend, but essential for you to know. I'll get right to the point. The access is changing…frankly, it's closing. Very soon the music will not be able to guide anyone to Kashdune—or back to the other side."

Joe stood up immediately. "Are you saying we can't leave?"

Felix jumped up too. Sweat began soaking through his shirt. "What about Dad?"

Stumpworthy held up a hand to quiet them. "The citizens of Kashdune have decided to prevent travel between the two sides. They felt a strong need to safeguard their island from being exploited by people from the other side. Several years ago, they began to implement their plan. First they communicated with everyone who knew about Kashdune, giving them a choice to stay on the other side or come back here. Next, they destroyed all known references to the island."

Joe clenched his fists. "By blowing up Turkish caves! That almost got us killed!"

Stumpworthy narrowed his eyes. "Yes, that was unfortunate."

Joe glared back at him, remembering that this man was once a friend—but a friend who had tried, on several occasions, to destroy him. "Unfortunate that we survived, you mean."

Horace Stumpworthy straightened, meeting Joe's eyes. "My dear friend, I had nothing to do with the destruction of the cave; that was Fredrick's doing. If you recall, I was… ahem…indisposed at the time. As I understand it, he only wanted to destroy the references to the island that were recorded in the cave art. I'm quite sure he didn't mean to harm you."

"So he must have taken the journals, too!" Harmony yelled.

"They were his to begin with. He only reclaimed his own property." Horace Stumpworthy took a deep breath. "May I continue?" Everyone nodded. "The last element of the plan was the most difficult. It is the only area where I have been involved. Fredrick saved me from my life as a lemming by giving me the Eternal Water. He brought me here so that we, along with Albert Easton, could try to alter the density of the access cloud, affecting how it carries sound."

Melinda looked up at Augustina. "Will the music go away?"

Augustina shook her head. "I don't know. I know about the plans for the island, we all do, but I had no idea they were so near to closing the access."

"I can answer your question, Melinda," Stumpworthy interrupted. "The music will always be there, but it will no longer be able to guide anyone through the access."

Felix felt weak and panicky. He placed his hands on the table to support his weight. "What will happen to people who follow the music?" he asked in a croaky voice.

"I can't say. Hopefully, they will turn back before entering the cloud, because once inside the mist…" Stumpworthy paused as he looked into Felix's eyes. "You can still get out from this side…for at least sixteen more hours."

Felix slumped into his chair. "What about coming here—can people still come here for sixteen hours?"

Stumpworthy met his gaze. "From our calculations, the access from the other side is already altered. If anyone were to follow the music to Kashdune, my fear is that they would never make it through that cloud—either to the island *or* back to the other side."

Chapter Twenty-Six

Felix and Melinda were out of breath by the time they reached the marina. "What does Meike look like?" Melinda panted, slowing to a walk as she stepped onto the wooden dock.

"Like a faun," Felix answered, gasping for air.

Melinda eyed him suspiciously. "A baby deer?"

Felix stopped and stared at his sister. "A faun from mythology—a goat-boy," he chided, shaking his head.

Melinda ignored his tone and kept walking, looking from side to side as if this goat-boy might spring at her at any moment.

"Hello," called a teenaged boy standing at the marina store a short ways ahead.

"Can you tell us how we can find Meike?" Felix called back.

"Course I can…you don't recognize me, do you? I'm Meike. Last time I saw you, I was in character for a play— Puck, if you recall—and you were looking for your sister. Looks like you found her."

Felix smiled awkwardly. Without his goat-like body and horn-topped head, he looked very different. "Yeah, sorry. This is Melinda."

"No worries. You missed a great play, but I understand that you were pretty busy."

"Sorry about that…"

"No need to explain. Everyone knows about Fredrick Hamsong's condition. News travels fast around here. I was on my way to get your boat ready…heard you'll be leaving today."

"That's what we came to tell you," stuttered Felix.

Meike shrugged. "Augustina already sent me a thought. I take it you don't use telepathy yet."

Melinda smiled at his use of the word *yet*. "Sometimes I think I'm getting close. I was hoping that Augustina would teach me."

Meike nodded. "Yeah. It used to be the kind of thing your parents would teach you, but now we all learn it in school." Meike turned to face Felix. "That's it," he pointed toward the end of the dock where a large white yacht was moored, answering Felix's unspoken question. "That's the *Nautica*, Mr. Stumpworthy's boat."

Felix's face flashed crimson.

"You can take a closer look at it if you want, I'm sure he won't mind, seems like a nice enough bloke." Meike winked at Melinda, then started walking away. "I've gotta go—it's going to take some time to get those two boats ready, and I promised Mr. Stumpworthy I'd have them both seaworthy in a couple of hours."

"Both of them?" asked Melinda.

"Yeah," Meike called over his shoulder as he trotted off. "He'll lead you out to the access to make sure it's safe to travel through, because of all the changes."

As soon as he was out of sight, Melinda rounded to Felix. "I know what you're thinking!"

Felix had been looking in the direction of the *Nautica* and turned slowly toward Melinda. "So what am I thinking?" he asked, his voice heavy with exasperation.

Melinda gave him an opened-mouth grin. "You were thinking about changing into Stumpworthy!"

Felix reeled backward, catching his balance just in time and narrowly avoiding falling into the water. "Not you, too…tell me you didn't read my mind."

"This is so cool!" Melinda sang, jumping up and down. "I really did read your mind!"

Melinda settled down when Felix placed a hand firmly on her shoulder. "Okay, okay," he shushed. "You did it... now stop doing it, and listen. What I was thinking just then isn't important, but the feeling I'm getting about Dad might be." His voice trembled as he thought about his father. "He may be following the music to Kashdune. I've tried using my connection to tell him not to come, but I don't think he's listening. I don't know how to use this telepathic stuff." Felix looked out across the marina toward the horizon.

Melinda frowned as she followed his gaze. "If he is following the music, then he won't hear your thoughts. When I went through the access, I didn't think about anything except the music."

"That's what I was worried about," Felix groaned.

"So how's changing into Stumpworthy going to help Dad?"

"It's not. I don't even know why that flashed into my mind." Felix glanced back at the *Nautica*, then back at the sea. "Maybe Dad isn't really coming. I'm probably worrying for nothing, thinking about all the bad things that could happen with the access changing."

Melinda sighed. "Even so, I think you need to keep trying to send Dad messages. If he isn't listening to the music, he'll hear you and know we're coming back." She looked back toward Stumpworthy's yacht. "If he is following *He Aeros Musike*, then there's only one way we can communicate with him, and that's if I go through and intercept him—*before* he goes into the cloud."

"I thought you couldn't do that because you don't know the music from this side," Felix lamented.

"True, but someone around here does."

"Who? Augustina doesn't even know it. The only one that was going to be able to help was Fredrick."

Melinda's eyes flashed as an idea struck her. "Stumpworthy has to know the sound, because he's supposed to lead us out, remember? He'll lead us in the right direction until we all hear it and can follow the melody. I think he just wants to make sure we leave; he doesn't want us sticking around since he's living here now."

"Of course he knows it, but how are we going to convince him to give it to us? He could've explained it to us already, but he hasn't. And you know he won't help us if we tell him about Dad trying to get through. He hates Dad as much as he hates the rest of us."

Melinda blinked back a tear. "Yeah, he'd probably make sure none of us could warn him." She clenched her fists and then turned to face the *Nautica*. "I know! Let's check out his boat for references to the music."

"We can't just snoop around. What if someone sees us?"

"Like who? Meike already said we could have a look… we can tell anyone else that we have permission." Melinda grabbed Felix's arm and pulled him in the direction of the boat. "I can't think of anything better, can you?" Felix didn't answer, and Melinda didn't wait another second before sprinting away. Felix hesitated, looking back over his shoulder to make sure that no one saw them—then he too jogged over to see what they might find on Stumpworthy's imposing yacht.

Jake had been flying for hours, focused only on the magnificent music that would carry him to Kashdune. The air was still, the sun perfectly warm, and the sea below him was calm. He closed his eyes, confident that the music would guide him. So absorbed was he in the harmonies of Kashdune that he hadn't noticed that the wind picking up significantly. Nor did he pay attention to the increasingly violent swells and the water crashing below him as the sea erupted. Even his entrance into the cloudy mist didn't wake him from his migratory trance. His only thought was the music, reaching its crescendo in his journey toward Kashdune.

When she reached the *Nautica,* Melinda skidded to a halt. The gangway was down and the door to the cabin appeared to be open. She knew she could pop in and out quickly, but she was frozen on the dock.

Felix stopped at her side. He looked at her apprehensively. "I know what you mean," he sighed.

Melinda turned her head to look up at him. "I didn't say anything."

"I know you didn't," he laughed nervously, "but I know you're afraid to go up there." Melinda smiled and nodded as Felix continued. "Look, we'll be together. Even if Stumpworthy comes back, what can he do to us? We'll just say we thought he was here, since the door was wide open, and we wanted to ask him when we're leaving. Remember, if things get difficult, you can always turn into a tiger or that grizzly bear of yours. He can't transform anymore, so *you* have more power than he does."

Melinda smirked and puffed out her chest. "That's right...I do!" She leapt onto the gangway and ran up to the cabin, followed closely by her brother.

Once inside, Melinda's eyes sparkled with delight. "Wow, this must be like a movie star's yacht," she whistled. "That man may be evil, but he sure knows how to live." She wandered around the room, gaping. "How much money does he really have? He must be a bazillionaire." She looked over at Felix.

"There's no such thing as a bazillionaire," snorted Felix. "But I know he's at least a multimillionaire, maybe even a billionaire." Felix opened a large cupboard and began rummaging through it. "There are some papers and documents in here, why don't you..." He turned to see Melinda posing like a fashion model on a large sofa across the room. " Melinda! What are you doing?"

"I think this kind of life would suit me. When we get back, you go and get more money out of Stumpworthy's bank and let's buy a boat like this."

Felix grabbed her arm. "Get up, we don't have time for this. We've got to find those maps. Why don't you go up to the bridge and see if you can find some charts or anything that looks like musical notes. I'll keep looking here."

"Okay, okay, don't get huffy. Back in a second," she sang as she jumped to her feet and disappeared out of the cabin.

There was nothing that looked like a musical reference in the cabinet. Felix shut the door and turned to scan the rest of the room. It was very large and, as Melinda had said, it was impressive. There were three large, cream-colored sofas set in a semicircular arrangement. A large table was at the center of the circle, with only an old newspaper and a single book, entitled *The Science of Sound,* lying on top. There didn't seem to be any other written materiel in the entire room.

"There's got to be something here," Felix whispered to himself as he walked around, looking under cushions and beneath the furniture. Exhausting any possibilities of finding anything in the room, he stepped out into a passageway, opposite the doorway through which they had come in. It was a short hallway that led to two rooms, one on either side. On the right was a small stateroom, with a bed and an empty chest of drawers. Across the hallway was another bedroom, this one was very large, but still simply furnished, with only a large bed sandwiched between two small tables at the head. Two large built-in closets stood across from double glass doors that led onto a deck. There were no pictures, papers, or books.

Felix stood in front of one of the closets, holding his breath. Gripping the handle, he paused; a worried expression crossed his face and his hands began to shake. He took a deep breath and began to pull. "What am I afraid of?" he whispered as he exhaled. "The bogey man?" He squeezed the handle and tugged the door open, hopping back as he did. Only about a dozen crisply ironed shirts confronted him.

Felix was frozen in place, but not from fear. It was more a feeling of entering a time warp, as if he'd been transported back to Paris—back to that day, only a few weeks ago, when he found himself standing in front of Stumpworthy's wardrobe, deciding what to wear. It was the day that he had transformed into the image of Horace Stumpworthy in preparation for his visit to the bank. Choosing a shirt should have been a simple task, but at the time it had been daunting. Felix shook his head …the memory seemed like a lifetime ago.

"I think I found it!" Melinda screeched from the other room, bringing Felix back to the present and nearly knocking him off his feet.

Felix shut the closet door and called, "Let's get out of here. This place is making me feel really weird."

Melinda met him in the doorway, eyebrows raised and a smirk on her face. "I can see that."

"What are you on about now? We've got to get out of here and you've got to get to Dad." He pushed passed her.

Melinda followed, still giggling. "And you say my mind wanders!"

"What are you talking about?"

"You have changed into the professor again and you don't even know it!" Melinda clicked her tongue in disgust. "You had better change back to *you* so we can go."

Felix spun around, catching his reflection in the sliding-glass doors. "Oh my God! I didn't mean to."

"Now you know how I feel when I get antlers and tails. You can't let your mind wander or you change whether you want to or not. But never mind about that now—I've got the music and I can read it!" She hummed the first part of a strange melody. "Give me a minute, then I can follow the same music in the air. That should lead me through the access and, hopefully, to Dad. Then you had better change and get out of here before Meike comes to get the boat ready."

Melinda read through the pages, humming as she ran her finger down each one. "I heard a lot of this music when I was on my way to find you; that's when I found Joe. At the time I couldn't figure out how to put it together. It's really weird, isn't it?" She looked up. "It all fits together, even though it's not as nice as the other music I've heard."

It only took a few minutes to learn the melody that would carry her through the access. She shoved the sheets of paper into Felix's hand. "I'm going now. I'll find Dad and meet you on the other side. Keep sending your thoughts to him, and I will to Joe." She bounded out of the cabin and onto the stern deck. "Remember to take these clothes back to Augustina—they're Evan's—and tell everyone I'm sorry I couldn't say goodbye in person. They'll understand when you tell them about Dad." She closed her eyes and lost herself in her transformation, feathers sprouting up all over her body. She opened her eyes before completing the change. "See you on the other side!" When she closed her eyes again, she dissolved into a kestrel and flapped away.

Felix watched as Melinda flew out across the water. It didn't take long before she was nothing but a miniscule dark speck against the azure sky. "Okay," Felix said to himself. "I'd better get changed and go find the others."

"What was that?" a man asked from behind him.

Felix's knees buckled and he felt like throwing up. He gripped the wall to keep himself upright.

"Horace! Are you all right?" The man's voice was filled with concern.

Felix slowly swiveled around to see a short, balding man with beady black eyes staring at him through perfectly round eyeglasses. Felix smiled weakly and nodded.

"You don't look well, but maybe this will cheer you

up," the man smiled. "I brought you the latest computer analysis of the changes to the access. I'm pleased to say that congratulations are in order. As you know, I told Fredrick that it couldn't be done—but you, my friend, have proven me wrong."

Felix's mind was racing. He knew he was still in the form of Horace Stumpworthy, but if he opened his mouth, he doubted he could fool this man who seemed to know the professor rather well. The man was holding out a stack of papers for him to take, which he reluctantly did. Clipped to the top paper was a handwritten note simply saying, "CONGRATULATIONS!" It was signed "ALBERT". *Okay, don't panic,* Felix thought. *This must be Albert Easton, and he's human; he won't be able to recognize that I'm not Stumpworthy, at least not by looking into my eyes. I just need to keep my mouth shut!*

Albert Easton took a step closer, causing all of Felix's pores to release what felt like a gallon of sweat. "Take a look at page fifty-seven," he said. He grabbed the pages back, thumbed through them and then handed them back to Felix. "This is the most current data on the sound tests. You were right. The access was indeed altered about forty-eight hours ago. It's now official—the access is closed! You did it...and I, for one, am very impressed." The man looked puzzled at Professor Stumpworthy's lack of enthusiasm. "I'll leave it with you," he said hesitantly. "I'm going to collect the data you wanted from the other side of the island. I'll be back in a day or two."

Felix felt like his stomach was twisting into knots, but he managed a nod and a half smile.

Easton frowned, looking awkward as he turned slowly, his eyes still focused on Stumpworthy's face. "Are you sure you're all right?"

Felix nodded Stumpworthy's head.

Albert Easton shrugged and left the cabin.

Felix didn't move, still staring out through the doorway.

"What am I going to do?" he gasped. The access was already closed, and Melinda was on her way there now. Horace Stumpworthy was planning to lead the rest of them there very soon. He might be able to prevent that from happening to his group—but what about Melinda and their father? Joe could get to Melinda—he had to! "But Dad—we'll never see him again," he cried out. He spun around to leave, but found himself instead face to face with the real Horace Stumpworthy.

The professor stared unblinking into Felix's eyes. Then he began to laugh. "Very impressive transformation. I'm not terribly excited about the attire you've chosen for my body, but other than that you've really surprised me, young man."

Stunned by this sudden appearance, Felix turned around and attempted to run, only to be hit in the left buttock by a painful sting. Instantly he slumped to the floor and stared up as the professor walked around, looking down at him. He was holding a hypodermic needle, beaming with a delight that looked savage. "It's very similar to the Burungo sedative…the same that *you* used on me, if you recall. They don't have Burungo plants on this island so I had to get creative with some of the other plants that had similar properties." He looked down at Felix's frozen position and smiled. "Surprising how quickly it works, isn't it? It won't put you to sleep, and you will be able to keep your eyes open to see what's happening around you, although you won't be able to do anything about it. It's too bad you won't be able to help me name it…perhaps I should name it after you," he laughed, "Since you are the first person I've ever tried it on."

It was true. Felix couldn't move a muscle, but he was completely aware of his situation.

"It's too bad that you're such a clever boy, always sticking your nose into other people's business. If you weren't, I could have dealt with you along with the others. That way, when you all went into the access, you'd be together. One big, happy family in the limbo of the mist."

Stumpworthy sat down across from where Felix lay prone on the floor.

"I do hope you're comfortable down there," he sniggered. "Since you don't appear to be in too much of a hurry, let me tell you a little story. The first part involves my coming here and being prepared for you. We can thank good old Albert Easton for that. I saw him only minutes ago, leaving the boat. He nearly wet himself when he saw me walking up the dock but poor dumb human that he is, I easily talked around how I could appear to be in two places at once. So you see, I knew that someone was on my boat, masquerading as me. Luckily I had some of the sedative with me. You see, I had loaded a few syringes as a precautionary measure, just in case I might need it to make your family's journey through the access more comfortable."

Felix glared up at the professor with a mixture of loathing and terror.

"Don't worry, my boy. I'll take care of the rest of your family. They'll join you in the access very soon. What a lovely reunion you'll have…if you find each other in that impenetrable cloud, that is." He smiled hatefully. "After I'm rid of you and your meddlesome friends, I can take care of Fredrick. And of course I'll take care of Augustina, too. She is a lovely woman, don't you agree? She'll be mine soon enough, with Fredrick's condition deteriorating daily. Frankly, I'm surprised it's taken so long. I thought that after I had altered the Eternal Water he would die a lot more quickly. If the Hamsongs had replenished their supply of Eternal Water, instead of relying on the water that I… let's say *enhanced*, Fredrick would have recovered instantly. They're much too trusting on this island, you know."

Felix was screaming in his head, but he couldn't do anything to stop the madman in front of him.

Stumpworthy looked up and saw Meike on the dock making his way to the *Nautica*. "Won't be a minute." He smiled at Felix. "I'll just inform my young friend of our change of plans."

He sauntered out of the cabin and called to Meike from the bow of his boat.

"Meike, no need for you to ready the *Nautica*—I'll take her out and check to see that she's okay for the journey, if you would be so kind as to untie me. When you've finished readying the other boat, you can send for the rest of our party. Felix and Melinda are with me. Tell their mother and her friends to meet us at the one-mile marker. The children were excited to ride in my boat for at least part of the journey. What could I do? I promised I would give them the ride of their lives."

He waved Meike away and then gave in to a deep chuckle as he stepped back inside to where Felix lay helpless.

"There we go, all set," he said cheerfully. "Once I get rid of all the irritants on this little paradise, I can take over. You see, I'll still be able to travel through the access by following the new sound patterns I've established. In essence, dear boy, there will be only one person in the world that holds the musical key to Kashdune…and that person will be me."

CHAPTER TWENTY-SEVEN

"Are you absolutely sure that's what has happened?" Elaine paced the terrace while Augustina explained what Meike had told her.

"He said he talked to Felix and Melinda at the marina. They were very interested in Horace's yacht, and he saw them get onboard. Soon afterward, he saw Horace. Meike said he untied the boat and watched as it left the harbor."

Elaine shook her head. "I'm just having a hard time believing they would go off with that man, after everything he…"

Augustina stopped her. "I'm sorry, Elaine, but you must learn to trust again. We don't have these kinds of problems on Kashdune because we have learned to live with each other rather than fighting. Melinda and Felix may have felt an unusual kind of excitement and curiosity about Horace. You will be together very soon."

Joe and Harmony listened to the exchange, each wearing the same concerned expression.

Augustina turned to Joe. "Are you sensing anything from Melinda that should cause concern?"

Joe looked at Elaine. "Actually, I'm not. I can sense that a feeling of excitement has replaced her anxiety. This might be a good thing, since she was reluctant to leave Kashdune on such short notice. A lot has happened to her in the last few weeks—a lot for an eleven-year-old girl. She may need a little excitement to get her through things."

Elaine shook her head. "I don't feel good about this."

"Horace will take care of them just as he is taking care of Fredrick and me," Augustina said. "He has been so good to me, staying by my side during this difficult time. I don't know how I would have coped without his strength."

"Elaine, if it will make you feel better, I can fly out and join them," Joe offered.

"I'm probably being silly," Elaine smiled, "but that really would make me feel better."

Evan was sitting on the grass, away from the terrace where the adults were discussing Melinda and Felix's departure. He had been consumed by his father's illness and hardly paid any attention to Melinda or her family. He looked down at the strands of grass that were crumpled underneath his bare legs, leaving an intricate pattern imprinted on his skin. He remembered sitting on the grass with Melinda a few days earlier. She'd called it 'grass tattoos'. Evan smiled solemnly. It was strange to think that his new friend might be gone forever. Everything was moving so quickly, with complicated changes taking place without warning.

He stood up, then walked through the middle of the adult conversation. No one took any notice of him as he scooted across the terrace and into the house. He took very little notice of them. He was in a dreamlike state, set apart from this strange reality. He wondered for a second if he had become invisible. A quick glance at his hands told him he hadn't.

Inside the house, he felt eerily alone. This was the only place he had ever lived, but today it felt cold and strangely foreign. He wandered down the hallway, past paintings and plants, tables and tapestries. Nothing offered him the usual sense of security; nothing felt as welcoming as it should. It was almost as if he was floating through time and space, only remembering sensations, not experiencing them. He thought for a moment that this was how it must feel to be a ghost.

Evan wandered through the house, never stopping or even pausing. He didn't have a destination in mind as he followed the invisible homing device that tugged him along. It really wasn't much of a surprise that he wound up in his father's room. He stood in the doorway for several seconds, staring unblinking at the prone shape in the bed. He looked at his father with a detachment that he had never experienced before—probably because the figure in the bed didn't even resemble his father. Fredrick Hamsong's dark hair was now almost white; his firm, rugged face had become deeply lined, and his once healthy complexion was sallow and frail.

As Evan tried desperately to understand his father's plight, he began to feel again. But he didn't feel anxious or sad. He felt angry. He was angry at his father for dying. He was angry at the access for changing and taking his new friends away. He was angry at Horace Stumpworthy for making it so. But most of all, he was angry at Melinda.

When he remembered their first meeting, he seethed. He had helped her when she was in need. She had been alone and frightened, and he had taken her to his home, where he and his mother cared for her. They gave of themselves—and now? When he needed her, she had simply left. No thank you, no goodbye. She had deserted him again without even a passing thought.

Evan sat in the chair he'd placed next to the bed and took hold of his father's lifeless hand. It was so unfair and cruel; whatever was doing this to his father was unjust. His father had been a good man and tried to help people. Why couldn't anyone help him now?

He thought about Melinda, happily cruising on that glorious boat, laughing and perhaps gorging herself with ice cream. Why wasn't she here? Didn't she care about his father? Why was she only concerned about herself?

Evan's anger was boiling. His hands were shaking and his teeth were grinding. "Melinda!" he hissed, "you should be here to help us. We helped you and your family, but you only think of yourself!"

Miles out over the sea, Melinda was almost at the access. The winds were beginning to pick up, and the water below was changing rapidly into a rumbling, inhospitable sea. The music had, at first, been difficult to follow. Its tones and pitches didn't flow beautifully together. Instead, they were forced into a cacophony of musical vibrations. But it wasn't this jumble of melodies that upset her concentration. While the music attempted to pull her forward, her mind experienced an unfamiliar interference, like sunspots affecting TV reception, or electrical storms cutting off power supplies. Strange, hostile feelings hit in rapid succession, upsetting her balance and distorting the music. It was like a war inside her head, with the harmony of the access being challenged by an angry enemy that was pummeling each note. Melinda was flying erratically as she fought to maintain the balance of the symphony, but she was losing it, the remaining shreds of the melody lost in an unfathomable tangle of sounds.

She opened her eyes and realized that she had obviously flown off course. The air was again calm and the sea returned to its glassy smoothness, with only the gentle, rolling swells as a reminder that it was a powerful force. She flew in every direction, trying in vain to pick up the remnants of the music to guide her. The fragments that she could hear didn't fit together. She circled back in the direction of the island and called mentally to Felix: *I've got to try it again. I'll have to go back to the beginning. Felix, keep trying to reach Dad…tell him I'm coming!*

The *Nautica* cruised smoothly out of the harbor with its happy captain, Horace Stumpworthy, humming the tune of the access. "Well, Felix, it's a beautiful day for a little cruise, don't you think?"

Felix had stopped listening. He remained motionless, slumped on the floor. He had taken refuge in his own world and his own thoughts. He had failed to protect his family and friends. He had been so stubborn about using his Athenite abilities, when he should have spent time honing his skills—at least developing his connection to his father. If only, if only...

This time Stumpworthy had won. He would finally succeed in destroying the Huttons, obliterating Joe Whiltshire and rubbing out Harmony Melpot. What drove a man to such evil? Could power really push a person to such lengths? Felix looked up at the smiling professor. Horace Stumpworthy's wickedness defied a simple explanation. Yet part of it was surely the poison of hatred that had infected his soul.

It's all over, Felix thought, resigned. *I wish it wasn't so... but I'm the only one who knows anything, and what am I to do?* He mourned the loss that he was about to suffer and prepared himself for his eventual end. His family and friends were doomed. *If only I could warn them. I wish I could tell Augustina about her own future,* he thought fleetingly. How could anyone protect her after Fredrick was dead? She was strong and could take care of herself, he knew. But she was also trusting, and might not be a match to Horace Stumpworthy's mastery of manipulation. If only she would disappear and stay that way for a long time.

Felix closed his eyes, remembering the watery image of Augustina as she swept by the table. He lost himself in the memory, trying to imagine the feeling associated with transforming into...nothing. The clarity of thought and freedom of movement must be the zenith of perception. He breathed in deeply, feeling comfortable for the first time since his ordeal began. He felt free from the thoughts about his captor and the fate of his loved ones and, for the moment, accepted the world as it was. *Dad,* he called through his mind, *I wish I could see you again. I would like to tell you that I will always respect and admire you and that I love you.*

"Well, well, well…the constantly morphing boy!" Horace Stumpworthy laughed as he looked down at Felix, or at least what remained of him. Felix had achieved the ultimate transformation, having vanished from sight. All that was left were his clothes wrapped around his invisible body, gently expanding and contracting with the intake of his breath. "You have done it again, dear boy—but learning to vanish won't help you. The sedative is too strong even for that unique transformation to overcome.

"I have to admit, I'm envious. I would have liked the challenge of learning these skills. But my time to learn such things is over, thanks to you and your lovely family. Stuck in the body of a lemming was no picnic, laddie. And the cure! The Eternal Water! Now what am I? I can't transform. I can't learn all the many gifts of an Athenite. If it weren't for my mental abilities, I would be almost a loathsome human.

"I don't expect you to understand. But maybe after you float about in that lovely cloud for a while, you'll realize you have brought this upon yourself. And some mistakes, my boy, will haunt you for the rest of your life."

Jake Hutton had been flying for hours. He had no choice; the music was controlling his desires, and his only thought was to follow its pull. He was deep inside the access, following the melody that would no longer lead him to Kashdune, though he could not know it. All he knew was the music. He would fly until he could no longer move, and then…? He didn't think about such eventualities—the music was his guide, a power he trusted with his life.

Occasional calls penetrated his thoughts, tiny voices vying for his attention. Each one was pushed aside by the strength of *He Aeros Musike*. But those stubborn little whispers grew into shouts until Jake could no longer shrug them aside. Soon their pull equalled the force of the melody and, for the first time in hours, Jake paused. He held his position, hovering in midair. The cries inside his head now outnumbered the force of the harmony that had held him captive for so long. He pushed against the pull of the music of Kashdune to follow a very different call.

CHAPTER TWENTY-EIGHT

Horace Stumpworthy cut the engines just outside the area of convergence for the old access. Only a few meters away was the impenetrable cloud that, as yet, remained hidden from view. It was unmistakable, the smooth swells replaced sharply by the choppiness of a restless ocean. For Felix, it was time to face his mortality. Stumpworthy smiled down at the heap of clothing that identified Felix's position.

"You wait here while I get things ready," he snickered. "Won't be a minute."

Felix listened intently as the professor clunked down the steps and trotted out onto the main deck. It was difficult to tell what exactly he was doing, but Felix heard scraping, clanking and finally splashing.

The professor returned in short order, smiling sinisterly. "Felix, your transport is ready. Don't worry—you won't have to do a thing. I will adjust the controls on the lifeboat so you'll travel directly into the access; you won't even have to listen for the music. And don't worry about getting the boat back to me, it's yours for the rest of your life." He laughed maniacally, then grabbed Felix by the shirt, slipping his arm around the boy's invisible waist. "Up you go! Let's make this quick—I still have your mother, Joe, and Harmony to ferry out here." Felix closed his eyes, shivering at the plight of his loved ones.

Stumpworthy struggled as he tried to lift Felix's invisible and limp body, dropping him several times in the process. Felix might have lost his power of movement, but his senses were keen and he felt every painful bump and jab. He groaned inwardly when the professor lost his grip, sending Felix slamming back to the floor and knocking his head painfully against a cabinet. Finally the professor gave up trying to lift him, and Felix wanted to scream out in pain as he was tugged across the floor and sent bouncing and thumping down the stairs to the cabin, falling in a heap at the bottom. Stumpworthy picked him up by his feet and dragged him across the floor. Felix's head thudded against the raised threshold of the deck.

If it hadn't been for the bruises and his incredible headache, Felix might have enjoyed the feeling of the fresh sea breeze when the professor dropped him on the deck. He remained in that position for several seconds, feeling the rocking of the boat in the rippling water before opening his eyes. Squinting at the brightness, he recoiled slightly at the feel of a spray of saltwater that tickled his face. It was strange, he thought, to feel so relaxed when he knew his doom was imminent. Calmly he recalled his first encounter with the access. It hadn't been that long ago, but it felt like an eternity. He knew this time would be different. The window of the access would take him again, but to where was the unanswerable question. A shudder swept through his body, and he prayed that the magical passage might at least reunite him with his family.

Horace Stumpworthy laughed with glee, like a child presented with an unexpected surprise. "This is wonderful! We've got company," he sneered, pointing to a shark's fin that was circling the boat. "If by chance you don't make it into the access, it looks like you may be able to contribute to nature in a different way. In this case you'll be but a simple link in the food chain!"

He grabbed Felix by the shirt and pulled him to the side

of the *Nautica* before pushing him overboard. Felix had one moment of stomach-clenching free fall before he thudded into a hard-bottomed little boat, hitting his head painfully against the side. *That's what that noise was—he was lowering the lifeboat,* Felix thought.

Stumpworthy climbed in after him, kneeling in front of the small outboard motor. He clasped a T-shaped handle and pulled the ignition cord until the engine fired and puttered into gear. "There we go—not a bad little boat, eh, Felix? I'll just lock in your course and get you pointed in the right direction," he said cheerfully. The boat began pulling against the line securing it to the *Nautica*. Stumpworthy turned the rudder eastward, then gradually accelerated. "We'll need to pull the *Nautica* around so that when I loosen your line you'll be traveling on the correct route." The engine strained and smoked as it tugged the larger boat into position. When the professor was satisfied with the course he had set, he slowed the speed. "Now, don't be impatient; you'll be going a bit slowly, but you'll get there. I've already tested it on a few other dinghies."

He sighed loudly and frowned at Felix.

"You know, Felix," he said calmly, "I know what you and your family think of me, but I want you to know that I have never killed anyone. There's never been a need to, since people seem to manage their own deaths quite nicely. Like you and your family—you'll die in your own time, and probably by your own doing. It might be longer than you realize, because we have no way of knowing what will happen in that cloud. Of course, if our little fishy friend here is extra hungry, your life might end sooner rather than later. Life is always a gamble, don't you agree?"

Happy with the direction he had set for Felix's journey, Stumpworthy turned to climb back up the ladder. As he raised his foot onto the first rung, the small boat rocked violently, knocking him to his knees. His happy expression melted into disgust.

"Watch your step, boy—I don't know how you managed to do that, but don't try it again."

At once he realized that he was shouting rubbish, as Felix was clearly incapable of any such movement. Regaining his footing, he prepared to climb up to the *Nautica* when another jolt upset the boat, forcing him onto his back and nearly throwing him into the water.

"How is this…?" He didn't even finish his thought before a third jarring impact shook the little boat. He jerked round again to stare at Felix, when he caught sight of the shark's fin rapidly approaching. With no more than a second to prepare, he braced himself, crouching on the bottom of the boat. "So it's you, our man-eating amigo," he snarled after the shark had passed. "Don't be so eager—you'll get your meal in due course."

The shark seemed to be preparing for another pass at the lifeboat. Stumpworthy scrambled to his feet and leapt up the ladder only seconds before the beast hit again, this time causing the outboard motor to stall.

"You stupid, prehistoric abomination!" he screeched from his safe perch on the *Nautica*. He glared at the shark, now circling away from the boat, racking his brain for a way to deal with Felix now—then an idea surfaced that caused his face to break into a wide smile, and he melted into laughter. "Okay, my sharp-toothed comrade. You win!" He scurried back down the ladder and grabbed Felix firmly. Then in one great thrust he threw him into the water with an enormous splash. Horace Stumpworthy wiped his hands against his trousers. "That was so much easier. I don't know why I bother with such complex schemes… the direct approach is always the best."

The moment that Stumpworthy grabbed him, Felix sensed what was about to happen, and the sensation as he hit the cool water wasn't shocking. Unfortunately, he was still paralyzed, so swimming to safety wasn't an option. He breathed deeply and floated on his back as he calmly assessed his situation. *I can't move, not even to grab hold of the boat right next to me, and there's a rather hungry shark a few meters away. Could be worse, I suppose, but I don't know how.* Felix was surprised at his cool detachment despite his precarious circumstance. He didn't know whether the sedative or his invisibility was his saviour but whatever it was it might just save his life. He knew he could float in the salty water and the fact that he was invisible coupled with his lack of movement might discourage the shark.

The shark made another pass at the lifeboat, rubbing against Felix as it did. Felix felt his heart explode into a violent rhythm as his breathing was jolted into a staccato of gasps. He mentally thanked the sedative, which at least prevented him from thrashing about. That type of movement would surely signal the shark that lunch was served. The shark continued to circle, coming in very close, but not close enough for a sample of the invisible morsel that floated helplessly only inches away.

Horace Stumpworthy was watching from the deck of the *Nautica*, eagerly wondering when the stupid beast would get on with its meal. "I should just get out of here," he murmured to himself. "But what if that shark doesn't eat the invisible boy? I can't risk his body being found after I was so careful to let everyone know that he was with me." He turned and stormed into the cabin, returning a short time later clutching a large knife. "Maybe a little blood will give that monster a clue that its food is right in front of its nose!"

By the time he reached the deck, Felix had drifted a few meters away. "Hold still, you stupid child," he hissed as he climbed down the ladder and into the lifeboat.

He started the engine and slowly negotiated the choppy water to where he could see Felix's clothes floating on the sea. As he drew alongside, he disengaged the throttle into its sputtering neutral position and then leaned over the side in an attempt to slash Felix's leg.

"I should have brought a hook or a harpoon," he cried,

when he hit only water. "And the waves are getting bigger...
that means we're too close to the access." Again he leaned
out to stab at Felix, but the choppy waves, with Felix sliding
down one as the boat was climbing another, made contact
impossible. Stumpworthy slumped into the boat to catch
his breath. "I should just leave him—if he's not eaten, he'll
probably drift into the access on his own, or drown, and
then I'll be rid..." Stumpworthy didn't finish his thought
as the huge fin swept by, only inches away from his small
boat. "Get him, you moronic fish!" he screamed as the
shark made straight for Felix.

The shark swam rapidly toward Felix, but once again
it didn't attack. Instead, Felix was swept into its wake and
pulled back in the direction of the *Nautica*.

Stumpworthy shook his head. "Don't play with your
food! There are starving sharks all over the world! You have
food handed right to you—don't waste it!" He slumped
inside the boat and exhaled loudly. "I need some blood to
entice that monster to eat the boy. But I guess it doesn't have
to be his blood."

His face was contorted with madness. Gripping the
knife in his right hand, he held up his left arm and stabbed
the tip into his forearm. It was more painful than he'd
expected, and he howled, lunging forward and dropping
the knife. Blood spurted out, covering his arm and tinting
the water at his feet a brilliant ruby hue.

The shark circled closer.

"Now we've got your attention," Horace laughed. "I'll
just drip a little bit of my blood around the boy to whet
your appetite."

He glanced around to locate Felix, who was floating
even closer to the yacht.

"Stupid currents," he ranted, fumbling with his good
arm to engage the motor. The little engine clicked on
for an instant, only to stall a second later when the shark
bumped the boat, splashing water into the motor. "Blast

you!" he seethed. He looked back at the *Nautica*, where Felix was now floating right next to the ladder. "I can't believe this is happening," he grumbled. "Impossible— the currents are taking me in the opposite direction!" He pulled and tugged on the starter cord, but the engine only gave a sickly whine.

Felix's ears were submerged in the water, but he could still hear the muffled sounds of Stumpworthy's voice. He felt the water whip around him as the shark swam past, rubbing its leathery skin right up against him but not bothering to attack. He was too relaxed to care about either of them. He could barely focus enough to keep mentally calling out to his father, who did not answer.

Stumpworthy was growing increasingly frantic. Each second that passed sent him farther into rougher water. He was still only a short distance away from the yacht, but he realized to his horror that he was drifting very close to the old access.

"I've got to get out of here! The new access is miles away…no one can make it out of this one anymore," he screeched. He fumbled and tugged at the ignition, only to be rewarded with a splutter and a choking sound. *There's too much water splashing into the engine!* he thought, pulling the ignition cord in vain.

As the first wisps of mist encircled his tiny boat and the sea slowly smoothed out, he noticed the terrifying approach of that huge shark. He looked back at his yacht, hoping that at least Felix would not be there, that he'd been eaten or drowned. His hopes were dashed when he caught a glimpse of his clothing, still floating next to the ladder.

The shark was swimming directly at him; its enormous mouth was open, its rows of sharp white teeth glistening in the sparkling water. The blood was leading the predator right to him. Horace Stumpworthy threw back his head in a howl, more animal than human. His exquisite life flashed before him and hysterical grief washed over him. "THIS

CANNOT HAPPEN TO ME! I AM PROFESSOR HORACE STUMPWORTHY!" he yelled at the top of his lungs.

Horace Stumpworthy closed his eyes for a moment in utter despair, then opened them and stared defiantly at the shark. He reached for the ignition, pulled it firmly only once, and the engine came to life. He pushed the throttle to full speed and the boat lurched forward.

"I have won! I will escape your wicked jaws because I am beyond you all!" he cheered. Then he looked ahead and realized he was travelling on a course set to enter the access. "There's still time," he panted as he turned the rudder to the left.

The shark veered to cut him off. Horace moved the rudder back in the other direction, trying to outwit the stupid fish, but the shark stayed a step ahead, always just intercepting him. The boat was travelling in a zigzag line, and with each deviation, the shark forced Stumpworthy to pilot back the way he had come. He screamed shrilly, realising he was traveling straight into the access. He turned in a last-ditch effort to avoid both the shark and the access, staring directly into the eyes of his attacker.

"YOU!" his voice thundered. "MELINDA HUTTON! HOW COULD YOU…"

Those were the last words Melinda heard as Professor Horace Stumpworthy was swallowed by the mist.

CHAPTER TWENTY-NINE

Meike stood on the dock, looking out toward the harbor entrance. "There it is! The *Nautica* has just entered the channel," he called to Elaine and Harmony, who were sitting anxiously on a small bench in front of the marina office, just a few meters away.

Elaine sprang to her feet, wringing her hands. "Thank goodness. I was getting worried. Joe left hours ago to find them. I was just about to transform and go find them myself. I'll be more comfortable having Felix and Melinda travel with us and not that horrible man."

Harmony smiled as the boat came into view. "Meike, I'm curious—what did Horace say when he radioed in?"

Meike shrugged. "I didn't talk to him. Melinda is the one who made the call, and she just said they'd be coming back. She was telling me that your friend Joe was with them and to make sure that you didn't leave the island. To be honest, I'm not used to communicating on the radio. We all use telepathy around here. Mr. Stumpworthy usually just sends me a thought when he has a change of plans."

"Horace uses telepathy?" Harmony gasped.

Meike nodded. "He seemed to learn very quickly. I suppose that when he lost the ability to transform, his other senses got a lot stronger...like when someone loses their eyesight and their hearing gets better." Meike started walking in the direction of the *Nautica's* berth.

Elaine followed. "Did Melinda say anything else?"

Meike's face flashed crimson and he looked down at his feet. "She was talking really fast and I couldn't understand what she was saying. Then something weird happened to the blooming radio…smoke started spewing out and everything."

"What's happening out there?" Harmony shrieked, pointing a shaking finger at the incoming boat.

Meike and Elaine jerked round to see what had attracted Harmony's attention. The *Nautica* was well within the channel, following a somewhat erratic course. They watched in alarm as the yacht narrowly missed colliding with an ancient Viking longship. Having avoided catastrophe by only a few inches, it staggered away, veering to the left and almost careening into the side of an antiquated Spanish Galleon. Then, at a speed never before seen in this peaceful harbor, it raced directly toward the dock.

"What in the world is he doing?" Meike screeched. "He's brought his boat in a hundred times and I've never seen him driving like this!"

"He's going to ram the dock!" Harmony yelled. "I knew he wanted to get rid of us, but I never thought he'd use his boat as a weapon!" She tugged a horrified Elaine off the dock, followed closely by a very baffled Meike.

Seconds before impact, the *Nautica's* engine squealed and cranked. Still moving forward, albeit more slowly, the yacht bounced off a wooden piling, shaking the entire dock, then backed off, seemingly on a collision course with a two-hundred-year-old British frigate moored a few meters away. The engine groaned again and the yacht lurched forward, this time at an angle to the wharf. Now moving at a speed a snail could easily overtake, the boat manoeuvred against the dock, scraping the weathered wooden pier. Elaine covered her eyes, Harmony covered her ears, and Meike covered his wide-opened mouth as the large yacht struggled into position.

The engines were cut and the *Nautica* gently bobbed in its own wake, banging rhythmically against the pier. The once sparkling new yacht, now bearing a thick brown stripe down its side where it had rubbed against the wharf, remained silent for several seconds. "Must be something wrong," Meike said as he cautiously crept back onto the swaying dock. Elaine and Harmony, looking equally bewildered, followed close at his heels.

Elaine stopped dead in her tracks when she looked up at the person who had been driving the boat. "Joe?"

"Careful!" Harmony chimed in.

"I never claimed to be good at this, but I got us here safe and sound," Joe called out as the boat's hull scraped against the wharf.

Melinda, struggling to throw a line to Meike, took up the call. "We'll explain everything later. First we have to get to the Hamsongs' and save Fredrick!"

The garden at the Hamsongs' house was peaceful. A chorus of birdsong enhanced the music that lingered in the air, and the myriad of dazzling flowers swayed gently in the light breeze.

"I can't believe this has happened." Augustina shook her head; her expression was filled with happiness as well as regret. "He completely fooled me…I thought he was a friend."

"Horace Stumpworthy was a master, all right," Joe said. "You're not the first person to have fallen for his charms and not seen the true wickedness of his nature."

Fredrick Hamsong, now with permanently white hair, his face lined and aged, gave a small smile. "I'd like to say something good about him, but I'm afraid nothing comes to mind at present. What I can say is that we mustn't hold onto our anger as he did. We have seen firsthand what carrying around that kind of hatred will do to a person." He paused, staring out across the garden. "I don't know how I'm going to break the news to Albert. He's a very trusting man, and very easy to manipulate. He had developed a real admiration for Horace."

Harmony looked over at Felix, who had finally recovered his mobility but, while his general outline could be now discerned, was still a bit transparent. "What I don't understand is how you and Melinda connected."

Felix looked up. "When I was completely invisible, I felt stronger mentally than ever before. I was always calm, even when I was thrown into the water. I could think clearly about everything, and instead of my emotions controlling my reactions, my brain took over—like a computer that finds the best solution to a problem within seconds. Melinda and I had already begun to use a little telepathy, but it was so much clearer when I was invisible. The strange part is that we didn't connect until she was on her way back to the island. I don't know what kept her from flying into the access."

Melinda smiled at her brother and then turned to Evan. "I think it was Evan who actually turned me around. I followed the melody for a long time, but something made it impossible to concentrate and I lost the music. I didn't realize what happened until I saw Evan when we arrived here. Then I remembered all the angry thoughts that surfaced in my mind; they were so strong that I could no longer hear the musical impulses guiding me. I guess Evan was *really* mad at me." Evan blushed brilliantly and Melinda continued, "When I began flying back to the island, I tried using telepathy to tell Felix what had happened."

"I sensed that Melinda was okay, but to be honest I didn't know where she was. I wondered why the shark kept bumping into me but didn't attack. I thought maybe I was just keeping still enough. There I was thinking the sedative saved my life, when all the time it was my sister." Felix paused and shook his head. "I tried to reach Dad, but I couldn't."

"I wouldn't say that," Jake said, rocking everyone to attention. He sauntered out onto the terrace, wearing some of Fredrick's clothes that just about fit perfectly. "In fact, you saved my life." He looked around at the gaping stares that greeted him. "I'm sorry—I didn't mean to startle you, but I've only just arrived, and instead of greeting all of you as a falcon, I thought it best to tidy up at bit." He turned to Fredrick and Augustina. "Hi, I'm Jake." He reached out, shaking their hands. "I hope you don't mind that I've helped myself to some of your clothing."

Augustina looked at him with wonder. "I didn't even know you were here! What is happening to my senses?"

As Felix and Melinda tackled their father with hugs, Fredrick massaged his temples. "So you're saying the access is still open from the other side."

"I'm afraid not," Jake lamented. "I was flying for hours in that cloud, following the music that wasn't leading me anywhere. Then another, more powerful impulse attracted me. It was Felix, reaching out with everything he had. His emotions proved a more powerful pull than the music."

Fredrick chuckled softly. "Horace always said that the Huttons are a group not to be messed with lightly. Tell me, Melinda, how exactly did you make Horace go into the access?"

Melinda looked nervously around at the smiling faces on the terrace. "I didn't mean to," she said sheepishly. "It's just that every time I tried to cut him off one way, he turned the other. I was actually trying to herd him back to his boat but I couldn't. The next thing I knew, he disappeared. I dived straight down into the water and circled back the other way so I wouldn't be drawn into the access, too."

A Cheshire cat smile flashed over Felix's translucent face. "When she got back to the *Nautica*, Joe was already there. He was hanging off the ladder, poking at the clothes he saw floating next to the boat…which, of course, turned out to be me."

Joe shrugged. "Sorry about that." Joe shook his head at the memory. "Dragging a limp human body, especially an invisible wet one, out of the water and then up a ladder is no easy task."

"Yeah, and I've got the bruises to prove it," Felix smirked.

"What took you so long to find them?" Harmony asked.

"I was trying to follow Melinda—but as I learned later, she wasn't with the boat. I caught up to Stumpworthy about the same time she did. I saw Horace in the little dingy as this huge shark tailing him. When he disappeared into the access, I flew to the boat to check on the kids. When neither was on board I panicked—then I saw the clothes floating near the boat and the big dorsal fin of that huge shark making its way straight for them. It only took a few seconds to recognize Melinda the shark-girl, and from the way the clothes were filled out, I suspected that Felix may have learned Augustina's little vanishing act." Joe looked over at Elaine, then at Jake. "You should be very proud of your children. Their ability to harness their Athenite powers saved all our lives."

Fredrick clapped his hands. "Yes, my wonderful friends. You have saved us and protected Kashdune from the exploitation of a very evil man. He alone knew that the access had been changed to another sequence of musical notes. When I have been able to decipher the new navigational guide to the island, I will make sure that you have the key. Your friendship will always be cherished, and the gates to Kashdune will always be open to you."

Acknowledgments

Thank you to my family and all the wonderful people in my life who continue to encourage and support me. Heartfelt thanks to my agent, Fiona Spencer Thomas, who has been my rock over the years.

Thanks again to all the readers—Sam, Ian, Barbara, Tess, Emily, Lawrence, John, Kaitlin, Jo, Nick, Kevin, Travis, Charlotte, Chris, and Cindy—who offered their critiques, which helped steer *Key to Kashdune* to its final version. And to the wonderful people at MP Publishing, Mark, Alison, Michelle, Briah, Brandy, and all the others who worked so diligently to publish this book.